The Boy in the Shadows

Brenda passed a partially open door. In the opening stood a tall, good-looking boy with black, unruly hair. His eyes were dark and inscrutable, yet they seemed to be penetrating right into her very soul.

When their eyes met, Brenda shivered. His physical presence was powerful, almost overwhelming; and his piercing gaze made her feel strangely vulnerable. All at once Brenda felt uncomfortable, almost apprehensive, and she very nearly stumbled in her effort to take her eyes from his.

Who is he? she asked herself when she managed to make it back to her seat without falling.

Whenever she looked at the door, she saw the boy hidden in the shadows, and her thoughts became confused. She wondered if anyone else had seen him, and then realized with a start that he was standing in a spot where only she could see him. Was he doing that on purpose? "Who are you?" she whispered to herself again and again.

COUPLES

Books from Scholastic
in the **Couples** series:

Coming Soon...

BAD LOVE

M. E. Cooper

BANTAM BOOKS
TORONTO · NEW YORK · LONDON · SYDNEY · AUCKLAND

BAD LOVE

A Bantam Book   0 553 17368 5

Produced by Cloverdale Press Inc,
133 Fifth Avenue, New York, NY10003
Bantam edition published 1987

Reproduced, printed and bound in Great Britain by
Hazell Watson & Viney Limited,
Member of the BPCC Group,
Aylesbury, Bucks

Chapter
1

Dumb! Brenda told herself, shaking her head at her own forgetfulness. She and Brad had a picnic date, and she had forgotten to make the cole slaw. Which, she thought, wasn't too bad considering that she'd spent the entire afternoon preparing potato salad and fried chicken the way Brad liked it.

With her legs hooked on the bed, and her back pressed flat upon the shag carpet, Brenda played with the dangling turquoise-and-silver earring in her left ear. Brad had given her the beautiful long earring on the last day of school and, from the minute she had put it on, it became the only earring she ever wore in her left ear.

The telephone rang, interrupting her thoughts. Because it was the summer, and she was working more hours at Garfield House, Brenda's stepfather had given her a private telephone. He'd told her he was doing it because she was spending so much time on the regular phone, counseling the runaways.

Brenda had immediately seen through Jonathan Austin's stern explanation. She had realized that he was giving her the telephone not just because he was proud of her work, but because he was proud of the way Brenda had worked at becoming a real part of their family. It had been one of those rare times when she had felt a genuine rush of love for her stepfather, and had hugged him warmly. She had promised him that the phone would only be used for her counseling work, and, of course, for Brad.

Smiling at her memory, she picked up the almond-colored phone.

"Hello?"

"Hi, Brenda," came Brad's very tired voice.

"Hi, how are you?"

"I'm okay," Brad began, but Brenda interrupted him.

"Sometimes I'm dumb," she said quickly. "I got everything ready for the picnic and I forgot the cole slaw. But we can pick it up on the way to the park, right?" she asked cheerfully.

"Brenda — "

"I can't wait for tomorrow. We've had so little time together since school ended."

"Brenda," Brad said, louder this time.

Brenda stopped herself. Her eyebrows knit together. A frown tugged at the corners of her mouth. "What?" she whispered.

"I have to work tomorrow. They changed my schedule again. I'll be off in three days, not tomorrow."

2

Not again, she thought as she shook her head in an effort to deny Brad's words. Tears misted her vision, and she fought to stop herself from crying.

"I really am sorry, Brenda," Brad said sincerely.

Holding the phone a little away from her ear, Brenda stared at the ceiling and tried to calm down. He's not doing this on purpose, she reminded herself. Stay in control.

"Brenda?" Brad asked. "Did you hear me?"

Brenda sighed. "I heard you," she said at last. "Why can't you tell them you're busy? You're supposed to be off tomorrow. We made plans."

"I know we did. But I have to go to the hospital whenever they call. It's part of the agreement I made when I accepted the job and joined the program."

What Brad didn't say, and what Brenda knew, was that Brad's summer orderly job at the hospital in the preview to medical careers program would go on his school record as a college course credit.

"When I took this job, you told me you would understand. I mean," Brad went on, "you broke a date last week when you had to go to Garfield House for that emergency."

"That was one time," Brenda said defensively, remembering how upset the thirteen-year-old runaway had been. Brenda had spent three hours talking to the girl and convincing her to make one more try at working things out at home.

"I know I've had to cancel a few dates, but we can still have our picnic," Brad said in a brighter

3

voice. "My next day off is in three days. Brenda, no matter what happens, I won't go into work. I love you, and I'm really sorry about tomorrow."

Brenda's anger flew away in one long sigh. "I love you, too, Brad. But please, don't break our next date."

"I won't," Brad promised. "And I'm really tired, Brenda. They work us to death at the hospital. I've got to get some sleep," he told her.

Brenda relented when she heard how weary Brad sounded. "Okay. Sleep well," she whispered before hanging up and resuming her careful study of the white ceiling. "It's not fair," she told the ceiling. "It's just not fair."

Brenda wanted to be understanding, but in the ten days since Brad had started his job, he had cancelled four dates. Was it going to be like this all summer long?

Unhooking her legs from the bed, Brenda pushed herself away and stood up. She went over to her dresser, took off the silver earring Brad had given her, and put it on the earring tree next to Brad's picture. Looking at his face, she got a funny sensation in her stomach. They were so different on the outside, she sometimes wondered how she and Brad could have become a couple.

Brad's handsome face was capped with neatly combed straight dark hair; Brenda's long layered hair always seemed to be in disarray. Brad's deep brown intelligent eyes had a somber and thoughtful look that made him seem more mature than the other guys his age, whereas Brenda's large eyes and wide mouth were a reflection of her free-spirited gypsy image.

4

Not even Brad's chipped tooth could take away the serious and dedicated air that was so much a part of him. He always dressed neatly and conservatively, but Brenda loved to wear clothes that were more funky and far-out.

Together they looked like the odd couple, Brenda decided with a giggle. Miss Funky and Mr. Preppy. But amazingly enough they were not only a team, but a good team. On the inside, where it counts, they were alike. "Then why do I get mad at you?" she asked the photograph.

But Brenda knew the answer before she asked the question. She was angry with Brad because he had promised her that when school ended, and all his responsibilities on the student council were finished, they would have a lot of time together before he left for college.

Brenda had been counting on that time. During the school year, they were lucky when they had been able to eat lunch together. Brenda had envied her stepsister and Ted for all their time together. But the summer was supposed to have been different for her and Brad.

They had made plans to go on picnics, see concerts, and to have lots of evenings to just sit around and talk. But now it seemed as if they had even less time than during school. "It's not fair," she said again.

There was a knock on the door. Brenda turned just as her stepsister opened it. Chris, who was gently brushing her long blond hair, was wearing a pink silk nightshirt. She looked as perfect as always, Brenda thought, just like a model out of *Seventeen* magazine.

"Brenda, can I come in?" Chris asked with a radiant smile.

"Sure," Brenda shrugged, "pull up some floor," she told Chris.

After sitting down cross-legged on the bed, Chris gave her stepsister another smile. "All set for tomorrow?"

Brenda's stomach knotted, and tears began to fill her eyes. She turned quickly away from Chris, before her face could give her away. "I love going on picnics by myself," she said sarcastically.

"Not again," Chris moaned in sympathy.

Taking a deep breath, Brenda turned back to Chris. "Why don't you and Ted go? Everything's all set. I made the chicken this afternoon. At least you two can put it to good use. All you have to get is some cole slaw."

"I'm really sorry, Bren," Chris said gently, her large eyes moist with sympathy. "I really am."

Brenda swallowed hard. She smiled, trying to be a good sport. "It's all part of life, right?"

"I guess so," Chris replied. She hesitated, then in a different voice asked, "You're really mad this time, aren't you?"

Brenda felt the blood start to pound in her head. As she felt her self-control start to slip, she said fiercely, "Why shouldn't I be?" For a moment, there was silence. Then with a sigh, Brenda shook her head. "It's . . . I think I'm more disappointed than mad."

"Well, it's not as if he's dumped you for someone or something else," Chris said reasonably. "You know how important Brad thinks this job is. He wants to become a doctor, and college is so competitive. He figures this will give him an edge."

Brenda closed her eyes for a second before speaking. "I guess I wish that Brad was a little less dedicated to his future career, and more dedicated to the present — to us. But I do understand why he had to break our date." She shrugged her shoulders.

"I was just counting on being able to spend some real time with Brad before he goes off to college."

Chris reached out and took Brenda's hands in hers. "He's just being Brad," she said softly. "You knew what he was like from the very beginning."

Even though she still felt a little embarrassed by Chris's open, affectionate nature, Brenda squeezed her stepsister's hands and nodded. "Maybe that's why I love him," she admitted. "He has a purpose in life. If he wasn't as devoted to his ambitions as he is, I probably wouldn't be able to stand him. Besides, having the extra free time will give me a chance to work more with the kids at Garfield House."

"You really are a special person, Brenda Austin," Chris said admiringly. "I don't know if I would be so understanding if Ted kept breaking dates with me."

"Sure you would be," she told Chris just as the phone rang again.

Brenda grabbed the phone quickly, hoping that it might be Brad calling back to say he would find some way to take tomorrow off from work. But

7

it wasn't Brad, it was Carla, a fifteen-year-old runaway she had been counseling for the last few months.

"Hold on," Brenda said to Carla. Covering the mouthpiece she glanced at Chris. "It's Carla."

Chris nodded. She understood it was a private conversation and started out of Brenda's room. At the door, she turned back. "You and Brad really are alike, you know. You're just as devoted to Garfield House as he is to his future career. And thanks for the picnic stuff."

After Chris closed the door, Brenda uncovered the mouthpiece. "What's wrong, Carla?" she asked.

"Everything! It's all getting real bad again. I want to move back to Garfield House."

"What happened?" Brenda asked, her concern for Carla pushing away all thoughts of her disappointment with Brad.

"I can't talk about it on the phone. Can I meet you tomorrow?"

"Sure," Brenda said, realizing that it wouldn't matter what she did tomorrow if she couldn't see Brad.

"Oh thanks, Brenda. You're a really good friend. You're always there for me."

"Hey, no problem. But listen, the best way you can thank me is to hang in there with your family and work at it. Then tomorrow, you tell me everything, okay?" Brenda said. Then in an encouraging voice, she added, "Don't worry, Carla, everything will work out. Just don't do something stupid."

When she hung up the phone, Brenda felt depressed again. She loved her volunteer work at the halfway house, but she had been counting on a pure fun day tomorrow, a day off from the troubled atmosphere of Garfield House. Still, she was needed there, and it was better than doing nothing.

"Isn't it?" she asked out loud as she turned to look at Brad's picture.

Chapter
2

Monica was walking on air. Her feet were so far above the sidewalk she felt as if her Reeboks never once touched the ground. And it was all because of one phone call. Monica chuckled to herself, feeling a renewed surge of excitement as she thought about the call she received that morning from Charles Ross, the station manager of WRRK. The call in which she'd been offered the job as disc jockey for K-100's summer show, Teen Beat!

Monica began humming to herself as she walked. A month before school had ended, she had received a letter from K-100, telling her that the station was inviting all the area's high school female disc jockeys to apply for the job. Monica didn't think she had a chance in the world to get it, but she'd filled out the application anyway and sent in the tape of one of her shows.

Then, during the last week of school, Annie

Ross, a bubbly red-headed sophomore, had come up to Monica and introduced herself. She had told Monica that her father was K-100's station manager, and that she told him she thought Monica would be perfect for the station's teen show. Annie had also confided that her father wasn't easily swayed by anyone, including his own daughter, so it would be Monica's test tape that would get her the job. "But I know you're good enough to get it," Annie had added warmly.

Monica had been astonished that the station manager's daughter had even known who she was — after all her boyfriend Peter Lacey was the head DJ and star of the high school's radio station. But she'd hidden her surprise and thanked the younger girl. Even with Annie's support, Monica still hadn't believed she had a chance to get the job.

"But I did get it!" Monica cried out loud.

"What are you talking to yourself about?" Kim asked. The girls were helping deliver some desserts to a party that Kim's mom was catering. "I sense something's going on, and you'd better not hold back from me!"

Monica smiled self-consciously. She wanted to sound adult and professional, but before she knew it, she blurted out, "I'm going to be the DJ for Teen Beat!" She looked at Kim expectantly. So far she'd only told one other person her good news, her boyfriend, Peter Lacey.

"You got it!" Kim cried happily, her green eyes sparkling beneath her wire frame glasses. "Wow! That's great!"

"I know. I can't wait to start," Monica said,

11

pleased that her best friend shared her excitement.

"When is the first show?"

"Sunday after next. It's from ten to eleven."

Kim stopped suddenly.

"What's wrong?" Monica asked, almost dropping one of the dessert boxes.

"We're here," Kim explained, looking up at an old Victorian house surrounded by a yellow picket fence.

"Do you have to stay long?" Monica asked.

Kim shrugged. "An hour or so to help set things up."

Monica piled the three boxes on top of the rest. "Come over to the sub shop when you're done."

"I will if I can," Kim said as she started toward the house. "Hey," she called to Monica, who had started away.

Monica turned. "What?"

"Congratulations."

"Thanks," Monica laughed. With a wave and a smile, she called, "See you later."

The sub shop was humming. All of the tables were filled with kids from Kennedy High. Everyone was talking about what they would be doing for the summer. Invitations to parties flew from table to table. The giddy excitement of being free from school was reflected in everyone's voices and expressions.

The latest Talking Heads single was playing on the antique jukebox. The deep bass of the music made the motorcycle hanging on the wall vibrate crazily.

When the song ended, a girl put a quarter into the old jukebox and a milder song took over. With the noise level a little lower, Monica took a sip of her diet soda and leaned back in her chair. She smiled affectionately at Peter Lacey as he took another bite of her cheeseburger. Having finished his own burger five minutes before, he had started on hers. But Monica didn't care, she wasn't hungry at all. She didn't think she'd ever be hungry again.

"I still can't get over it. I wonder why they picked me?" she asked for the tenth time.

"Beats me," Peter mumbled, his eyes studiously fixed on the cheeseburger. "Mind if I have some?" he asked, reaching across the table for Monica's soda.

Monica nodded absently. Her mind was racing a mile a minute. "K-100. My own show," she whispered.

"Everyone deserves a break," Peter said, draining half of Monica's soda before giving it back.

"Yeah, but I never would have thought it possible."

"Hey! I'm a good teacher," he told her. Monica giggled at the look of false hurt on his face.

"I guess I'm lucky that they wanted a girl to do the show this summer."

"Lucky," Peter echoed.

"Annie Ross told me that she really pushed her father to choose me," Monica confided.

"Who's Annie Ross?" Peter asked.

"She's a sophomore. Her father is Charles Ross the — "

"Station manager for K-100," Peter finished for Monica.

"Right," Monica said, not surprised that Peter would know that fact. As far as she was concerned, Peter was an expert in everything and anything to do with radio and music. "I sent him a tape of one of my Friday shows, but I didn't think they would want me. When he called me today I nearly fainted."

"You're good, Monica," Peter reassured her, before smiling brightly and taking another drink of her soda.

Monica looked into Peter's green eyes. She suddenly felt a rush of gratitude, as she remembered how much Peter had helped her. "The only reason I got the job is because of you."

"You have talent, Monica. If you didn't you wouldn't have lasted two minutes as my assistant," Peter said honestly.

Peter's words were reassuring, but Monica still felt uncertain. She looked down at her hands. "I'm really scared though, Peter."

Peter reached out, covered her hands, and squeezed them gently. "Don't be. You're going to have a great show," he said encouragingly.

"I hope so," Monica whispered, enjoying his touch.

"I need another soda," Peter stated. "Can I get you one?"

Monica shook her head. She watched Peter walk up to the counter and wait to be served. While he stood there, she felt a thrill just looking

14

at him. Peter was her good luck charm. Ever since they had gotten their relationship straightened out, everything had been going right for her.

It hadn't started out that way. Shortly after becoming Peter's assistant at the school's radio station, she noticed the undeniable attraction between them. Monica had believed they were in love, until she'd discovered that Peter was going out with Lisa Chang, a beautiful ice-skater training to be in the Olympics. The knowledge came too late, because by the time she found out about Peter's long-distance relationship with Lisa, she was already madly in love with him. Monica had been horrified and ashamed of her feelings, and of the way she had behaved at the station with Peter.

Then something miraculous happened. Monica and Peter got locked in a closet together at the radio station, and after that, nothing was the same! Monica couldn't stop herself from blushing when she thought about the kisses they'd shared while locked in that closet together, waiting for someone to come and let them out. This time she was saved by Kim Barrie who just at that moment entered the sub shop.

"There's Kim," she said to Peter, relieved at being able to change the subject. "I saw her earlier and asked her to come by, if she could get away from work."

Waving to Kim, Monica motioned her to their table. She watched the way Kim's long, slender legs carried her so gracefully, and once again wished that she was as tall as her friend.

"Hi. Can I join you guys for a few minutes?" Kim asked, coming over to their table. "Mom gave me a short break from work."

"Sure," Peter said, "but you have to buy me a soda."

"You've already had three," Monica said with a laugh.

"I'm trying to drown my sorrows by getting a sugar high."

"Sorrows?" Kim asked as she sat down. Monica looked at Peter, puzzled by his remark.

"I thought this was a celebration," said Kim.

"It is," Monica stated. "I told Kim about the job," she said to Peter.

"Must be hard to keep good news like that all to yourself." Peter held up his soda glass in a toast. "See? I've created a monster," he joked.

"You've created a star," Kim corrected him.

"I doubt that," Monica cut in, pleased by Kim's words, but confused by the tightness she had detected in Peter's voice. "It's just a six-week show, one hour a week."

Smiling, Peter looked from Monica to Kim. "You should have heard her two minutes ago."

"That's not fair," Monica protested, her face turning ever redder.

Kim laughed and tilted her head toward Monica. "Can you believe this is the same Monica Ford we all *hardly* knew? I remember when Monica was so shy she wouldn't talk to anyone."

"She's changed a lot," Peter agreed, returning his gaze to Monica.

"She has," Kim agreed. "I think it's great."

16

Monica was pleased by their compliments, but unnerved by them at the same time. "Hey, can we talk about something else? You guys are really embarrassing me," she admitted.

"We're only telling you the truth," Kim said encouragingly. "What kind of a show is it going to be?"

Monica leaned forward, her hands clasped together on the table. "I haven't worked it all out yet. But," she said, taking a deep breath, "I don't want it to be like that guy they used last year. All he did was try to sound like a big-time DJ, and played only the big hits. I would like to mix public service stuff — things for kids — with good music. Maybe even an interview once in a while.

"What do you think about that, Peter?" Monica looked at her boyfriend eagerly.

Blinking, Peter looked into Monica's eyes. "Oh, um . . . it sounds like a good idea to me." Monica smiled. Peter seemed tired and a little preoccupied today. She hoped he wasn't having problems at home of some sort.

Kim stood up. "I've got to get back to the house. Mom needs me for another delivery."

"Are you going to work all summer?" Peter asked Kim.

Kim shook her head. "Not *all* summer. Woody and I have made a lot of plans. What about you guys?"

Peter shrugged. "I'm working at the record store four afternoons a week."

"Which leaves plenty of time for fun," Monica reminded him.

"That's what the summer is for. See you guys

later," Kim bubbled, before she swept out of the sub shop.

After Kim left, Peter quickly finished his soda. "I'm stuffed. How about going for a walk," he suggested.

When they stood, Peter took Monica's hand in his and guided her outside. At the corner, they turned onto a tree-lined street. It was a beautiful June day — warm and sunny, but not too humid. Summer was starting, she'd just gotten her dream job, she was in love with the most wonderful boy in the world — life was perfect, Monica decided. Monica felt at peace with herself.

"You really have changed a lot," Peter said, stopping them about halfway down the block.

As Monica looked up into his eyes, her heart began to beat faster. "In what way?"

"Every way. You're happier and you aren't running away from everyone the way you used to."

Monica couldn't take her eyes from Peter's. The hand Peter held felt as if it were on fire. Her lips were suddenly very dry and her heart was pounding. "If I've changed, it's because of you," she admitted, shyly. "And . . . because I love you."

Before the words were completely out of her mouth, Peter wrapped his arms around her slim back and drew her to him. His eyes looked dark and pleading as they searched her face.

"I love you, too," Peter whispered just before his lips covered hers.

"Peter," Monica asked a little while later, "will you help me with the show? Help me try to get it together? It would mean a lot to me." She was so full of energy and happiness that she felt she wanted to get started that very instant.

Peter stared at her for several seconds before he shrugged casually and smiled. "You know I can't say no to you."

Chapter
3

Brenda got off the bus and stepped into the warm sunshine. When she'd awakened, she had hoped that it would be a rainy day. At least then she wouldn't feel so bad about Brad having to cancel their picnic date.

But it was a sunny, beautiful day, making Brenda feel even more keenly her disappointment. Not really caring what she looked like, she'd thrown on a pair of cut-off jeans, a huge T-shirt that reached to an inch above the frayed hem of the shorts, and leather strapped sandals. She wore Brad's earring in her left ear, and three very different earrings in her right ear.

Although it was early yet, Brenda could tell it was going to be a scorchingly hot day. When she arrived at Garfield House, she paused to look around. The familiar wallpapered hallway was filled with small groups of kids, most of whom she recognized.

The three boys nearest her were dressed alike in jeans and T-shirts. They were in the middle of a heated discussion about a concert that had been on MTV last night.

Brenda walked past the group, saying hello to them by name. As she headed in the direction of the head counselor's office, she had to squeeze past the bunch of girls near the old Coke machine.

"Hi, Brenda," called a girl wearing black shorts and a loose white cotton top. "Are you going to be around later?"

Brenda nodded to the girl, whose name was Christine Andreas. "Problem?" she asked solemnly.

The girl shrugged, "Not really."

"I'll be around if you need me," Brenda reassured her, knowing that sometimes it could take weeks before one of the house residents could bring themselves to talk freely.

When Brenda reached the office, it was empty. She spotted a note for her on Tony's desk. It said that Carla had worked things out with her folks, and wouldn't be in today.

"Great!" Brenda said, pleased about Carla. But she had come all the way in for nothing!

"Isn't it," came the voice of Tony Martinez behind her. "I love it when one of *our* kids finally takes some responsibility for herself and does something about it."

Brenda whirled around to find Tony standing a few feet behind her. His curly hair and dark features were a perfect match for his muscular body. "It was a big step for Carla," Brenda said.

"I think you helped her to make that step. I'm

21

just sorry you had to give up your picnic date. I tried calling, but you had already left. There's still time to call Brad if you want."

Brenda shook her head. "He had to work today."

"That's too bad, but it helps me out," Tony said with a smile. "There's a special meeting of the city council about youth halfway houses. I need to be there to hear what they have to say. Want to take my group?"

Brenda's tongue froze. She stared at Tony for several seconds trying to recover from her shock. Tony's group was special. She had been part of that group at one time. It was made up of the hardest cases, the kids who believed they had no real home at all, except for Garfield House.

"Do you think I can do it?"

A smile formed on Tony's face, softening the rough features that made him look much older than he really was. His dark brown eyes sparkled. "Sure you can do it. You've spent enough time in sessions to know what to do. Just let them talk. Lead them, try to make them open up. Maybe they will because you're closer in age to them. I left the group member files on the desk for you to look over."

Brenda tried to smile. "Okay, Tony, I'll try. Uh, Tony?"

"Yeah?" Tony asked, as he gathered some papers together.

"Hey, you're not that old — you're barely twenty."

"Thanks," Tony said with a wink as he put the papers under his arm and left the office.

Brenda sat down at Tony's desk and nervously tried to think of how she would handle his group. Although she knew that a session usually ran itself, the responsibility to get the kids talking would be hers.

The Garfield House sessions were a form of group therapy, but they were special, too. In most halfway houses it was a professional therapist who was in charge of the sessions, but at Garfield House the youth counselors were in charge of the sessions. As head youth counselor, Tony Martinez ran most group therapy sessions. He reported to a psychologist, but it was Tony or one of the other counselors who did the real work with the kids. It worked because the kids trusted Tony.

"Will they trust me?" Brenda asked aloud, leaning back in the chair. She realized that Tony was giving her a chance to do something important, and she didn't want to blow it. "I won't," she stated before opening the first file. I'll make them trust me, she promised herself.

Brenda thought back to some of the group therapy sessions she had been a part of when she had come to Garfield House for help. The sessions were designed to make each of the kids feel as if they weren't alone, as if they were part of the whole group. Everyone's problems were brought out, and each member of the group would give his opinion of the other kids' problems.

An hour and a half later, Brenda had read all but one of the files. Just as she opened the last one, Theresa Simon's file, Tony reappeared in the office. "The city council meeting was canceled."

"Oh," Brenda said, both disappointed and relieved that she would not be running the session. "I guess I'll go home then."

"Come to the session anyway. There's a girl I want you to meet."

"Who?"

Tony pointed to the top file. "Theresa Simon. Did you read it yet?"

Brenda shook her head. "I was just starting it."

"Theresa ran away from her new home, and from her stepfather and stepbrother. Her case is a little like yours was."

Interested to see someone who was in the same situation she had been in, Brenda went with Tony. The group therapy room was the last room on the first floor, away from most of the other rooms. The walls were painted light blue, and two windows overlooked Garfield House's small backyard garden.

When they walked into the room, Brenda saw that the group was already waiting there. Eight chairs had been set in a semicircle facing a larger chair. Six of the eight seats were taken by four boys and two girls. Brenda thought that both girls looked as if they were around her age; all four boys appeared younger. Brenda moved one of the empty chairs next to Tony's, very much aware that the six kids were watching her carefully. She swallowed, her mouth dry. She felt excited, though, and eager to begin.

The first thing Tony did was introduce Brenda. Then he asked each of the kids to give Brenda a little of their history. Brenda knew it was one of the methods Tony used to make everyone a little more relaxed when there was someone new sitting in on the session.

Tony started with Bill Woods, the boy sitting on Brenda's left. Bill was fourteen, and had dressed in jeans and a T-shirt. He had long, dirty blond hair and smoky gray eyes that were already street-wise. But when he spoke, Brenda heard a little-boy quality in his voice.

When Bill finished his story, the next boy took over. And, by the time the second boy's story ended, everyone was paying close attention.

The room was silent for a few moments after the last boy had spoken. Brenda looked at the other kids. They all seemed to be lost in their own private thoughts until Tony spoke up. "Theresa, you're next."

Theresa Simon, the girl whom Tony wanted Brenda to pay special attention to, was one of the two girls in the group. Theresa was petite, barely five feet tall with dark, almost black hair, a pretty face, and pale blue eyes. She held her hands tightly together on her lap, and when she spoke, she looked down at them.

When she finished her very brief story, which did sound similar to what happened to Brenda, Brenda spoke up, "I can understand what you're going through."

"No you can't!" Theresa said, in a chilly voice. There was a shocked silence, as everyone in the room stared at Theresa.

Theresa glared defiantly at Brenda. "Who do you think you are to tell me you understand what's happening to me? None of you understand!"

Frightened that she'd done something wrong, and might possibly have hurt Tony's progress with Theresa, Brenda glanced at Tony. His expression told her that he wasn't upset, however. Rather, his eyes remained lively as he watched Theresa.

"Why don't you tell us what it is that we don't understand?" Tony suggested in a calm voice.

"No," Theresa said with a sullen shake of her head.

Tony nodded to Brenda. Brenda's mind raced a mile a minute. He expected her to say something! But what? She remembered the way she had been, when she had sat in Theresa's chair, and Tony had cajoled her into opening her heart to the group.

"If you can't tell us, then you have no right to be here," she told Theresa. From the corner of her eyes, Brenda saw Tony's nod of approval.

"That's right!" said one of the boys. "We try to help each other, not shut each other out."

"Talk to us," Brenda asked in a level voice.

"I . . . I can't," Theresa said, shaking her head sadly.

"Yes you can. All you have to do is trust us. It isn't easy. I know that. I had to do it myself. Theresa, let us help you. Not just me, but all of us. Please," Brenda pleaded, aware that she was overstepping her role but was unable to stop herself.

"I — " Theresa began, but she started crying and her words became muffled.

No one spoke, everyone waited until Theresa

started to speak again. "My father died a year ago. I . . . I really loved him. I thought my mom did, too. But how could she have if she married someone else so soon after?"

Brenda felt her own eyes fill with tears. It was hard to listen and not say anything. After drawing in a sharp breath, Theresa went on in a rush of words. "The man my mother married has a fifteen-year-old son. My stepfather doesn't understand me. All he ever tells me is to get better grades, and how much he hates my clothing and the way I wear my hair. But usually he just acts as if I don't even exist." It was an almost instant replay of her own life, Brenda thought.

"And my stepbrother . . . he never talks to me. We're in the same grade at school. He — he won't even let any of his friends talk to me. He is ashamed of me and he hates me. And I hate him!"

Theresa blinked several times and took a sobbing breath. "I just wish I was stronger."

Brenda walked over to Theresa and took the girl's hand. "It's because you are strong that you're at Garfield House," Brenda said. "It takes courage to come here and face the truth. If you didn't have that courage you would have . . . jumped out a window or something. That would be the easy way. Trying to work out your problems is the hard way. It takes guts."

"Wh-why d-don't I feel strong then?" Theresa asked Brenda.

"You will. I promise you that you will."

Theresa stared at Brenda for a moment longer,

then reluctantly, almost imperceptibly, her mouth turned up into a half-smile. Brenda felt encouraged. "When I first came here, I had a problem like yours. I never thought it would get worked out, but it did. You've got lots of help here. Everyone at Garfield House is here for you, just like they were for me."

Standing, Brenda released Theresa's hand. "Just remember that when you need to talk, do it — talk. Don't hold things back. No one will make fun of you, because we care about you. Okay?"

Theresa nodded. "Okay."

Brenda started back to her chair, passing the partially open door on her way. In the opening stood a tall, good looking boy with black, unruly hair. His eyes were dark and inscrutable, yet they seemed to be penetrating right into her very soul.

When their eyes met, Brenda shivered. His physical presence was powerful, almost overwhelming, and his piercing gaze made her feel strangely vulnerable. All at once Brenda felt uncomfortable, almost apprehensive, and she very nearly stumbled in her effort to take her eyes from his.

Who is he? she asked herself when she managed to make it back to her seat without falling.

The session lasted fifteen more minutes. But Brenda found it hard to concentrate. Whenever she looked at the door, she saw the boy hidden in the shadows, and her thoughts became confused. She wondered if anyone else had seen him, and then realized with a start that he was standing in a spot where only she could see him. Was he doing that on purpose? Who are you? she whispered to herself again and again.

But there was no answer, only a feeling of mounting fear and excitement.

Chapter
4

The employees' lounge was empty, except for Brad, who was taking a quick break before finishing his last hour of work. Sitting back on one of the green vinyl chairs that filled the room, Brad opened his can of soda with a loud pop. He was tired after his first six hours in the emergency room. But he had enjoyed it, because it had given him a real glimpse into the medical world.

The air conditioning felt good, and the low music coming from the speakers in the ceiling was soothing. The room was painted the same pale green as the rest of the hospital, but a full wall of windows helped make everything brighter.

He stared out the windows at the sunny day. "A picnic day," he said aloud.

Brad sighed. It had upset him to have had to cancel his date with Brenda. He'd been looking forward to spending the day with her. But he knew Brenda understood why he couldn't refuse to go into work. This summer was a chance to find out if he was cut out for medicine or if he was wasting his time. He didn't want to go through all the years of college and medical school if it wasn't what he thought it would be. Working at the hospital was the perfect way to find out if he really wanted to be a doctor.

And so far Brad loved the work. At this point in the summer, which was still pretty early, he thought that he did want to become a doctor and possibly specialize in emergency room medicine. But he had been working for less than two weeks, he reminded himself, and had barely scratched the surface of what went on in a hospital.

Brad glanced out the window again at the beautiful day and thought of Brenda. He was lucky to have her as his girl friend. Suddenly, Brad wanted to see Brenda. He missed her smiling face and throaty laugh. Standing, he started across the employee lounge toward the phone. He wanted to hear her voice, tell her that he loved her, and ask if he could come over tonight. When he reached the phone, he took out a quarter. He was certain that she would be at Garfield House, and decided to try there first.

Before he could put the money into the slot, the lounge door opened and Thomas Greer, the supervisor in charge of student orderlies, came in. He saw Brad and motioned to him.

"Davidson, we've just had two more no-shows. You'll have to work half of the next shift. Sorry," the supervisor said before walking away.

Brad said nothing, he just stared at his supervisor and put the quarter back into his pocket.

When the group session ended, Brenda stood slowly and smiled at everyone. Tony was the first one out of the room and, as the rest of the kids filed out, Theresa hung back.

"Could we talk sometime?" Theresa hesitantly asked Brenda when they were alone.

"Whenever you want," Brenda replied, and she meant it. "Are you staying here?"

Theresa nodded. "I'm in the second floor dorm. I have a room with Cindy and three other girls." Theresa paused to take a breath. "I wanted to thank you. I — I've had a hard time talking to the people here."

"It will get easier," Brenda promised. But she knew it might take Theresa a while. She had to be ready to open up and look at herself first, instead of blaming other people for what was happening to her.

"Thanks, Brenda."

"Sure." Brenda left the room and walked slowly down the hallway, feeling a sense of accomplishment at having gotten Theresa to take that final hard step. She silently prayed that Theresa's next steps would be easier.

"You were really super with that girl," came a boy's voice from behind her.

Brenda whirled around. She froze when she found herself face to face with the boy who had been watching her. Up close, his eyes were dark and smoldering and she felt trapped like a prisoner by the intensity of his gaze. They stood facing each other for several silent heartbeats before Brenda broke the spell and looked away.

He was a good five inches taller than she, and wore black jeans and a deep blue T-shirt. Brenda couldn't help noticing how his tight shirt accented his chest. His head was tilted to the side, as if he was carefully studying her slightest movement. For some strange reason, this bothered Brenda. Before he could speak, he took several steps toward her. His walk made her think of a prowling mountain lion.

Somehow she was able to free her tongue and speak. "You're not supposed to eavesdrop on group sessions," she told him with more forcefulness than she felt.

"I wasn't. I was watching you, and you were really good."

"If I was good, it was because I've been there myself." She replied abruptly, starting off down the hall. A voice inside her head was crying out run, but Brenda held her breath, hoping that he'd follow her. He did.

"I'm Jake Hoover," he told her in a husky voice as he caught up to her and fell in step beside her. "I just wanted you to know that I really admire you. I've been watching you around here. A lot," he added.

Brenda didn't reply, she couldn't. But when she reached Tony's office, she stopped and looked at Jake. She suddenly felt hot and was very nervous for no reason at all. The hall seemed close and stuffy.

"How long have you been here?" she asked, trying to ignore her unwarranted reaction to Jake.

Jake shrugged. The casual movement caused

her stomach to knot in anticipation. "A little while. I sort of check in and out."

"How come?" Brenda asked.

"I like my freedom," Jake replied with a smile as his eyes roamed across her face.

Brenda shook her head. "I meant why are you here?" It seemed as if Jake started to say something and then stopped. He gave her another smoldering gaze. "Problems," he finally replied. "Hey, I've got to split. See you later."

With that, Jake sauntered away, leaving Brenda to stare at his back. She leaned weakly against the wall, watching him until he disappeared.

"No," she whispered, afraid of sudden sensations that were swirling within her. Brenda denied her thoughts, trying instead to picture Brad. But all she was able to see was Jake Hoover and the hidden mystery in his eyes.

Think of something else! she ordered herself just as Tony appeared in the hallway.

"Hey, you were wonderful in there. I was very proud of you."

Gaining control of her runaway emotions, Brenda drew herself straighter. "I was afraid I might have messed up," she admitted.

"No way. That was the first time in three weeks Theresa's opened up."

"I'm glad I could help."

"So am I," Tony told her before giving her a brotherly hug.

"Tony," she asked nonchalantly when he released her from his bear hug, "what's Jake Hoover's story?"

Tony tensed. He stared at her for a second, and then grasped her arm and drew her into his office, closing the door behind them.

"What about Jake Hoover?" Tony asked as he went to his desk and sat down.

Unable to meet Tony's eyes, Brenda looked at the bulletin board on the wall. She carefully studied a notice for an English tutor. "I'm just curious. I met him a few minutes ago."

"To tell you the truth Brenda, I don't know much about Jake. He showed up here last week. He won't talk to me about anything. In the one week he's been here, Jake's been in and out three times."

"He seems okay. Maybe he just needs time," she ventured.

"He might seem okay, but I don't trust him."

Tony's words took Brenda by surprise. They bothered her because she'd never heard him speak that way about anyone at Garfield House. She thought of Jake, and of the strong aura that surrounded him. "Why don't you trust him?" she asked, turning to look directly at Tony.

Tony took a deep breath. When he let it out, he shook his head. "It's hard to explain. It's a feeling I get whenever I talk to him. He avoids all the sessions, unless I trap him into going. When he does attend a session, he doesn't participate. He'll listen, but he won't comment on other kids' stories, and he has yet to tell us something about himself."

Brenda nodded thoughtfully, realizing that Tony was being open with her in a way he would only be with the other youth counselors. She felt proud that she had reached a new level with Tony, but she still didn't understand why what he was saying about Jake bothered her so much.

"It's an act, right?" she asked.

"I think so. If I didn't, he wouldn't be here."

Brenda looked at the bookcase behind Tony. Her eyes traveled across the top row of psychology books. "What about his parents?"

"They were as hard to talk to as Jake is. When Jake first came, I called them to inform them that Jake was staying here. His father said he didn't care where Jake was, so long as Jake wasn't hassling him."

Brenda's eyes widened in surprise. She shook her head slowly. "No wonder Jake came here."

"That was my reaction, too. But when I spoke to his mother, I understood a little more. She said that Jake won't respect any of their rules. He comes and goes whenever he wants. He refuses to listen to his parents, and he resents any authority."

"Then he really needs our help," Brenda stated defensively.

Tony shook his head again. "I'm not sure if Jake Hoover belongs in Garfield House."

"I thought that anyone who came here for help belongs here," she challenged, shocked at Tony's harsh words. "You can't send him away."

"Think about what you just said," Tony instructed her. "The magic word is *help*. I don't think Jake came here for help. I think he's here because it's an easy place to crash without anyone hassling him."

"You can't give up trying to get through to

him, though," Brenda argued. "You never give up. Look at me."

Tony smiled. The lines of tension around his mouth eased. "You're special, Brenda. And it's because you don't think you are, that makes you special. One of Jake's problems is that he does think he's special."

"But you won't ask him to leave until you try to get through to him, will you?" Brenda pleaded.

Tony leaned toward Brenda. "No, I won't ask him to leave just yet. Now, let's talk about something nice. How's Brad, and what is he doing at the hospital?"

Brenda worked hard to make herself smile. "He's the same as ever. He's working all sorts of hours, and trying to plan out his fall schedule at Princeton."

"You two having fun this summer?" Tony asked.

"When he isn't working," Brenda admitted, no longer able to keep up her smile.

"Hey, what's this? My best girl getting down?" Tony asked in a teasing voice.

Brenda sighed loudly. "Maybe a little. It's just that I had planned on spending a lot of time with Brad, and it hasn't worked out — yet."

"You haven't been out of school for two full weeks, and the summer's just starting. Everything will be fine," Tony stated confidently.

"Sure. Sure it will be," Brenda replied. But deep inside she wasn't so sure.

An hour after she left Tony's office, Brenda was home, lying on a chaise in the backyard, reading a book, and enjoying the late afternoon sun.

On the outside she looked relaxed, but on the inside she was in a turmoil. Jake Hoover. Whenever she tried to think of Brad, her thoughts kept turning to Jake Hoover. She had to find out more about him!

Brenda was especially disturbed by the way Tony seemed to have already written off Jake. There was a similarity between herself and Jake that she couldn't deny. Tony said he was an outlaw. Brenda had always felt like an outlaw, too, at least until Tony had helped her realize what she had been doing to herself, how that kind of attitude had alienated her from others, thus perpetuating her loneliness and isolation.

Still, Brenda knew there was a little bit of the outlaw left in her. But she had learned that friends and family were important — too important to fight with and ignore.

"Hi, Bren," Phoebe Hall called as she strolled into the Austin's backyard. "I didn't think you'd be back this early."

"Back this early from where?" Brenda asked as she shaded her eyes from the sun and looked at her cheerful friend.

"The picnic," Phoebe smiled. "That's all you talked about yesterday. I didn't think you'd be back yet. I was looking for Chris."

"Chris is enjoying my picnic with Ted," Brenda told her in a low voice.

Phoebe's smile quickly faded. "What happened?" Phoebe asked with sudden concern. "Are you okay? Did something happen to Brad?"

"Yes," Brenda replied as she closed the book she'd been reading, "something happened to Brad."

Phoebe shook her head, her long red braid swinging vigorously. "Let me guess," she said disapprovingly. "Mr. Doctor-To-Be worked today, right?"

"You got it," Brenda said with a half smile.

Phoebe sighed and sat down at the end of Brenda's chaise. "Instead of getting smarter, he's getting dumber."

"It's important to him," Brenda said weakly, wondering why she was defending Brad when she agreed with Phoebe.

Phoebe covered one of Brenda's hands with her own. "You're supposed to be important to him, too."

"I am," Brenda replied defensively. "But Brad's got to think about the future."

"I know he does. We all do, but I hate to see you sitting around doing nothing."

"You know me better than that," Brenda scoffed, sitting straighter in the chair. "I handled an important group session at Garfield House today."

"That's great," said Phoebe. "You really are into that stuff, aren't you? Do you think you're going to become a psychologist?"

Brenda had never really given much thought to her future. In fact, it was only recently that she'd gotten her act together at all. But she considered Phoebe's question carefully. "I don't know," she replied thoughtfully. "I never even thought about college until I started going with Brad."

"Well," Phoebe said earnestly, releasing Brenda's hand, "I think you would make a good shrink."

"Really?"

"Yeah, think of all the money you could make — you could buy a big house with a tennis court and swimming pool, and the rest of us wouldn't have to get jobs at all. We'd just hang out and you could support us — "

Brenda threw the suntan lotion at Phoebe, and both girls burst into laughter.

"Hey, did you hear about Monica?" Phoebe asked as she tossed her red braid over her shoulder.

"No, what?"

"She got picked as K-100's summer disc jockey!" Phoebe burst out excitedly.

"That's great!" Brenda exclaimed. She was very impressed. "Maybe Monica will do some things for Garfield House."

Phoebe laughed. "See what I mean? You've got to become a shrink. You have a one-track mind."

"It's not that bad," Brenda protested.

"No? For a minute there, you sounded like Brad. Talk about one-track minds. Maybe you two have been going together for too long. You know what they say about old married couples."

For a moment, Brenda felt a flare of irritation. Because Phoebe had dated Brad for so long, she sometimes acted as if she knew him better than anyone else — including his current girl friend.

40

Even if what she said was true, Brenda didn't like to hear her joke about it.

She was saved by the sound of other voices. Turning, Brenda and Phoebe saw Chris and Ted walking toward them, holding hands and smiling happily. When they reached her, Ted bent and kissed Brenda's cheek. "I never knew you could cook. That chicken was outrageous!"

"Thanks," Brenda said, pleased that at least someone got to enjoy her hard work.

"But you've got to work on your potato salad. It was a little mushy." Brenda faked a punch at Ted's arm, which he easily ducked.

"It really was good, Bren," Chris added. Her long hair, which she'd piled on top of her head before the picnic, now tumbled down around her shoulders. Her face was flushed and she carried her shoes in one hand. Brenda looked at Ted and saw the same expression on his face. "It seems that you've been doing more than just eating chicken," she joked.

Chris blushed. Ted smiled.

"Jealous?" Ted asked.

All of a sudden Brenda *was* jealous. She needed to escape. "No," she whispered, unable to look at Ted. "I'm just hot. I need a shower." With that, she stood up, closed her book, and smiled at everyone. "See you guys later."

But she knew, hurrying into the house, that nothing would get rid of this empty angry feeling inside. Even worse, it was a feeling she was beginning to know all too well.

Chapter 5

"No, that isn't right," Monica groaned to herself. She stared at the three sheets of paper spread out on the kitchen table, and began to circle and then number certain items.

"What's not right dear?" Monica's mother asked, stepping into the kitchen.

Monica looked up to find her mother dressed in a crisp beige linen Dior suit. Her hair was swept up in back and she wore a three-strand freshwater pearl necklace.

"Hey, you look nice. Where are you off to?" Monica asked.

Mrs. Ford smiled. "I've got that fund raiser for the hospital," she reminded her daughter.

"Right," Monica replied, turning her attention back to the papers before her.

"You haven't answered my question, Monica," her mother reminded her.

"Oh, sorry — I'm trying to work out the program format for my radio show. You know, when to play music, when to make announcements —"

"Don't forget that you promised to make an announcement about the summer chamber music festival for the Arbor Foundation," her mother broke in.

"I won't," Monica promised, cringing inside. Chamber music on a rock show!

"Thank you. Well, good luck organizing your program and have fun today," Mrs. Ford said, giving her daughter a quick kiss before she waltzed out of the kitchen.

"Fun, ha!" Monica muttered in the direction of her mother's back. She was frustrated. Trying to put together a good program schedule for Teen Beat was harder than she had ever thought it could be. This was her tenth outline in two days, and still nothing seemed right.

Carefully, Monica tore a fresh sheet of paper from the pad, and began to rework her outline. When she finished, a half hour later, she scanned the page and nodded in approval. She got up to get a Coke, but when she sat down again and read over the outlined schedule a second time, a frown tugged down the corners of her small mouth.

"What's wrong?" she asked the paper before she looked at the phone and thought of Peter. Knowing that he had more experience than she, Monica decided to call him. It took four rings, but he finally answered with a sleepy hello.

"Boy are you lazy. I've been up for three hours," she told Peter.

"What time is it?" he asked, his voice sounding more alert.

"Ten-thirty."

"Ten-thirty!" Peter moaned. "It's summertime. There's no school. Mornings are for sleeping."

"I'm a working girl, remember?" Monica joked.

"Oh, right, I forgot," Peter mumbled, his voice sarcastic.

Monica was surprised at Peter's tone. Of course she had woken him up, and that could easily make anyone grumpy.

"Um, I'm sorry I woke you up, Peter, but I need help."

"With what?"

Monica sighed. She should be able to do this on her own, but she felt so uncertain and unsure. She respected Peter's abilities more than anyone she knew; he was the only person who'd know exactly what to do. And surely, being her boyfriend, he'd want to help her, to share in all the excitement.

"I can't make my program schedule work out right," she explained.

"Oh." There was a pause at the other end of the line. "What's messing up the format?"

"Well, for one thing, I can't figure out how to segue from the music into the discussion topics smoothly."

"What music will you be playing?" he asked thoughtfully.

"I don't know yet. Probably top 100."

"Okay, what you have to do is tie in the discussion topic with the music. Either pick the topic to suit the music, or the other way around."

44

Monica broke into a grin as she listened to Peter's words. "Boy, sometimes I'm really thick," she admitted. "I've been so worried about which records to play that I never connected the two things. I guess that's why it all looked so off. John Lennon doesn't go very well with a discussion about military careers, does it?

"That all depends on how you use it," Peter said. "But I would choose the music after I figured out the discussion topic. How long a segment will that be?"

"Fifteen minutes for discussion. Five minutes for public service announcements, five minutes for concert announcements, and the rest will be music," Monica stated.

"Sounds good to me," Peter told her.

Monica's spirits soared with pleasure at Peter's words. "Thanks, Peter, this really means a lot. I couldn't do this without your help. You know that, don't you?"

"Yeah, well, that's what I'm here for," came the voice from the other end.

"I'll come by Variety Records later, okay?" she asked. She wanted to thank Peter in person, and she especially enjoyed visiting him at the record store. The customers there loved him. Even though he was the youngest salesperson, he knew more than practically anyone else at the store.

"Sure, why not. It's been a little slow there the last couple of days," Peter said. His usually bouncy voice seemed dull, and again, Monica was concerned. Could something bad be going on in Peter's life that he just wasn't telling her about?

"Is everything okay?" she asked hesitantly.

"What could be wrong?" Peter replied abruptly. "Whoa," he said quickly. "I'd better get moving. I start work at one. See you at the store."

"Bye, Peter, and thanks again. I love you," Monica added in a low voice. When she hung up the phone, however, the feeling that something was wrong lingered. Whatever was bothering Peter was not something he was willing, or ready to share with her.

What could it possibly be? she asked herself silently.

Peter hung up the phone and exhaled sharply. "Why did it have to be her?" he asked the Springsteen poster on the far wall. Even though he'd just woken up, Peter didn't feel the surge of energy and excitement he usually felt when the day began. Instead, he felt tired. Shaking his head, Peter laid back on his bed.

He really wanted to feel happy for Monica, but he was having trouble. Ever since she'd gotten the job as the Teen Beat disc jockey, he'd been upset. But it wasn't her fault, he reasoned. Monica didn't know that for years he'd dreamed about working on the summer show that was always hosted by a local teenage DJ from an area school. He had never told her, of course, that he'd sent in an application and a test tape months before K-100 had announced the tryouts. He'd sent his material in extra-early, because he had wanted to get a jump on the competition.

"What competition?" Peter grumbled. He'd had his heart set on getting that job. He had daydreamed about how it would be the break that

46

launched him on his professional radio career. When the station replied to his application, the show's staff had written that even though they were impressed by Peter, they had decided only to accept applications from female students for this year's show.

Their decision was a blow, but it was something he could live with — or so he'd thought until he'd learned that they'd chosen Monica instead.

Peter closed his eyes. His feelings of resentment weren't logical. He *knew* Monica was talented. If she hadn't been, he wouldn't have taken her on as his assistant at the school station. But for some reason he felt betrayed by her. And he loved her, there was no doubt about that. The trouble was, it hurt to hear her always talking about *her* radio show. It seemed that all she did anymore when they were together was talk about Teen Beat, and K-100. He'd never said anything but sometimes Peter felt as if he couldn't bear it a second longer.

Every time she talked about the program, his stomach would twist with envy. Peter shook his head angrily and jumped out of the bed. "I'm going to drive myself crazy!" he declared. Then he looked around the room. "I am crazy, I'm talking to myself."

When a low rap sounded on his bedroom door, Peter turned. "Open," he called, wondering who it could be. His brother never knocked, he just barged in. And his parents were at work.

His question was answered quickly, as the door opened to reveal Woody Webster, wearing white jeans and a white crew neck shirt. "Yo, Peter," Woody said cheerfully, "I finally got that new computer filing program."

"Hi, Woody, that's good," Peter said. Then he did a double take. "What happened to your suspenders?"

"Good? You sound about as thrilled as if I'd said I was going to force-feed you brussels sprouts for the remainder of the morning — or is it afternoon now?" Woody replied.

"What kind of excitement is this? We've been talking about this program for a week." Woody paused to look critically at Peter. "As for my attire, I broke a snap on the suspenders. And if you want to get personal, isn't it a little late in the day for pajamas?"

Peter shrugged, and started to turn away. "Hey, are you okay?" Woody asked quickly.

"I'm fine. Just a little tired," Peter said with an evasive shrug. "Let's go set up the program."

"Peter, you don't get down too often. I mean, you're always in a good mood. What's bothering you?"

Peter was silent for a moment. "I thought you wanted to get that program going," he finally said.

"I do. But come to think of it, you've been acting a little weird for the last couple of days. Talk to me," Woody urged.

"It's nothing," Peter protested. "Really." Making himself smile, Peter took the envelope from Woody and opened it up. He slid out the thin spiral instruction manual, and pretended to study the cover. But he wasn't really seeing the colorful

48

multi-striped logo, or even the name of the program. All he saw was Monica's face, happy and animated, as she talked about her Teen Beat show.

How can I tell Woody that I'm jealous of my own girl friend? Peter wondered, feeling ashamed. "Woody," he began. Then just as suddenly, he changed his mind. He had to keep these feelings to himself. "I . . . I think this program is going to do what we want."

"Then let's go to work," Woody replied, giving Peter a strange glance. "That is if you like working in your pajama bottoms," he added with a laugh.

Monica hadn't lifted her head once in the two hours since she'd finished talking to Peter. When she finally did look up, it was because someone was banging on the kitchen door. With a sigh, she put down her pencil and went to the door. Opening it, she found Kim Barrie smiling at her.

"Oh, no!" Monica said, clapping a hand over mouth.

"Oh no what?" Kim asked when stepping inside.

"I forgot about tennis. I'm sorry, Kim, I've been so busy with my show."

"I think that you're becoming obsessed with this radio show," said Kim.

"What?"

"This is the summer, remember? We have no school, it's vacation and time to have fun. Have fun, Monica, okay?"

Monica stared at her best friend, surprised at

the way Kim was acting. Obviously Kim didn't understand. Nobody (unless she had been picked for this incredible honor) could possibly understand what she was going through. "You sound like Peter. He yelled at me when I called him before. He told me it was summertime, too, and that he wanted to sleep in the mornings."

"Why shouldn't he?" Kim asked, defending Peter. "He works every afternoon at Variety Records, doesn't he?"

"I know," Monica said with a shrug. "I'm just so involved with my show."

"Forget about it this afternoon, okay? Woody's meeting us after tennis, and I thought we'd all go over and hang out with Peter."

Monica smiled. The tight little lines that had formed around her mouth disappeared. "Maybe you're right; besides, with a little luck, I'll see something I missed when I look the schedule over later."

"Go change!" Kim instructed with a smile.

"Yes ma'am," Monica replied before dashing off to change. "Why don't you look over my script while I'm gone," she added from the steps.

It took Monica less than ten minutes to change and come back downstairs. When she glanced at the clock in the kitchen, she saw they would have just enough time to make their reservation at the Rose Hill Park tennis courts.

As they climbed into Kim's red Toyota, Monica said, "What did you think of the script?"

Kim shrugged. "I never saw a radio script before. But I can tell you've sure put a lot of work into it. There are so many little details in it. I never realized that every song's time was noted. I mean," she added, starting the car, "a show never sounds as orderly as it looked on your script."

Monica's smile widened. "That's the whole point of being so organized. In order for it not to sound that way, every minute of the show has to be plotted out."

"Has Peter been helping you with the script?" Kim asked.

"He's been wonderful."

"I'm glad to hear that. I was worried that he might not be handling it too well."

Monica was puzzled by Kim's last words. Her pale eyebrows knitted together and she stared at the road for a moment before looking at Kim. "Why wouldn't he handle it well?"

"No reason really," Kim hedged. "Forget I mentioned it."

Suddenly, Monica was irritated. "You did mention it," she reminded her friend, "so I can't forget it."

Kim squirmed in her seat for a moment, then finally sighed. "Don't take this the wrong way, 'cause I'm probably out of line anyway. But Peter's the DJ, you're his assistant. I know how much Peter wants to become a real DJ."

"But he's been great," Monica said. "Peter's been very understanding and supportive about everything."

"That's nice," Kim commented. "I'm glad I was wrong. See, I would have thought he'd be jealous. I know he applied to be the Teen Beat DJ last summer."

51

Monica shook her head slowly. "He never told me."

"Woody told me. I figured Peter didn't bother applying this year because the station wanted a girl."

Kim's words bothered Monica. All at once she felt uncomfortable. Peter's recent moodiness couldn't be related to her having been chosen as the DJ for Teen Beat? Or could it? Peter isn't like that, she told herself. If something was bothering him, she was sure he'd tell her.

"Wouldn't he?" she whispered.

"Wouldn't he what?" Kim asked as she pulled into the drive of Rose Hill Park.

"Nothing, I was just talking to myself."

"You've started doing that a lot lately. Is that what makes a good DJ, being able to talk to yourself?"

"You'd better watch it," Monica warned, "or I'll beat you so bad you won't ever pick up your tennis racket again!"

"Oh yeah?" Kim retorted with a smile. "We'll see about that. Winner buys a pint of chocolate Oreo ice cream?"

"You're on!" Monica laughed. As the two girls walked toward the courts, Monica forgot about Peter's moodiness and once again lost herself in the thoughts of her first radio show, which would be a week from Sunday.

"Ten days!" Monica declared.

Kim whirled around to look at Monica. "Not again," she cried.

"Sorry," Monica said, looking guilty, but the smile on her face told the real truth.

Chapter
6

"What, *again?*"

Brenda leaned against the office wall and avoided Tony's probing gaze by concentrating on the dumbbells he was using to do his midday curls. Because of the long hours Tony spent at Garfield House, Brenda knew that lunchtime was the only chance he had to keep up his workouts.

"I guess hospital work takes a lot of dedication," Brenda said, replying to Tony's question, but still not meeting his eyes.

"It does take quite a bit of dedication," Tony agreed.

"Can I do something for you today?" Brenda asked.

"You know we always need your help here," Tony replied gently. Brenda pushed herself away from the wall and stood straighter.

"Great. Then what can I do?"

Tony's features stiffened for a moment as he

said, "Well, I have one problem that I have to take care of personally." A moment later his face lost its intensity. "However, Theresa hasn't said a word since that session when you got her to open up a little. I was going to have a private talk with her, but since you're here, would you do that for me? Just hang out with her and try to get her to trust us some more. Can you handle that?"

"I'll try," Brenda said, eager to take on anything that would absorb her attention and get her mind off Brad. "She's living in the second floor dorm, right?"

"The middle room," Tony said, "your old room."

Brenda nodded and started out. "I'll see you later."

"Hold on," Tony called. Putting down the weights, he dipped his hand into his pocket and withdrew a handful of change. "Get two Cokes," he told Brenda as he handed her the money. "It's a good door opener."

Brenda nodded and turned, but Tony stopped her again. "Did you see Jake Hoover in the halls?"

At the mention of Jake's name, Brenda instantly became alert. "No. Is there a problem?"

"Nothing for you to worry about."

But Brenda saw the tense expression on Tony's face and wondered.

After getting two cans of diet Coke from the old machine, she went up to the second floor dorm. Because Theresa had not yet fully integrated into the life-style of Garfield House,

Brenda was sure she'd find her there and not with the other kids.

She was right. Theresa was sitting on her bed, staring down at her hands. Luckily, the room was empty.

"How do you like the bed? Does it still sag in the middle?" Brenda asked, stepping into the room.

Surprised, Theresa turned to look at her. "It's not bad."

"It's not that good either. Want a soda?"

Theresa looked at her with sad blue eyes. "Thanks." She reached out to take the can Brenda offered her.

"Can I sit?"

Brenda sat down next to the troubled girl and opened her can of Coke. But Theresa just stared at hers. "I spent a lot of nights sleeping in that bed." Brenda said. "But I couldn't stand looking at the walls during the day."

"They're okay," Theresa said listlessly.

"Sure they are, if you've got something bothering you so bad you can't see how ugly the paint chips are. What's wrong, Theresa?" Brenda asked.

Theresa shrugged again.

Frustration flooded through Brenda. Things didn't seem to be progressing. What could she *do* to get Theresa to talk? Maybe she should just concentrate on getting a casual conversation started. Perhaps once Theresa started to speak — even if it was about everyday things — it would be easier to guide her into the troubled area.

"What school do you go to?" Brenda asked, not looking at Theresa.

"I know what you're trying to do," Theresa said roughly, turning slowly to face Brenda.

Brenda openly met the girl's gaze. "What am I trying to do?"

"Shrink me."

Brenda shook her head, as her heart went out to the girl. "No, Theresa, I'm just trying to talk to you, because I want to help you, to be your friend." They stared at each other for a moment longer, before Theresa looked away.

"Why?" she asked. "I mean, I'm nobody to you."

"That's not true," Brenda protested.

"It's the way I feel."

Brenda nodded. She understood that comment perfectly. Theresa was just voicing the thoughts that Brenda herself had once lived with. It's hard to trust other people; it's hard, in fact, to like other people when you don't like yourself. Now if she could only get Theresa to realize that.

Brenda gently put her hand on Theresa's shoulder. "Tony asked me to talk with you because we've both been through similar things. I ran away from home after my mother remarried. I hated my stepfather and my stepsister. And I do know some of the things you're going through. Believe me, Theresa, I do."

"That doesn't make it any easier for me," the girl said.

"Have you ever tried to speak to your stepfather instead of running away from him? Have you tried to find out if the way he's acting is because he doesn't like you, or if maybe it's because he's not sure about how to handle a daughter?"

"But he doesn't like me," Theresa stated.

"Have you given him a chance to like you?" Brenda asked, remembering how hard it was for her to accept Jonathan Austin as her father.

"I — " Theresa began, but instead of words, a sob caught in her throat, and she began to cry.

Without hesitation, Brenda pulled Theresa into her arms. She held her silently for several minutes, her heart aching for the girl until Theresa's tears had finally subsided.

As Brenda gently stroked the girl's black hair, she felt a strange sensation at her back; someone was watching her.

Turning her head to glance in the direction of the door she had forgotten to close, Brenda saw with a start that Jake Hoover was standing there. His dark, brooding eyes were fixed on her and she shifted uncomfortably on the bed. Jake's intense gaze unnerved her, and she shivered at the way he so openly studied her. Brenda turned away from him and continued to stroke Theresa's head.

He had no right to spy on them, she thought angrily. And what was he doing up in the girls' dorm anyway? She wanted to shout at him to go away, but she didn't want to upset Theresa. Realizing that she was temporarily helpless, Brenda did the only thing she could. She ignored Jake, pretending that she and Theresa were alone. Later, she promised herself, she would have a stern talk with Jake Hoover.

A minute later, Theresa took a deep breath

and sat up. "I'm sorry, I didn't mean to — "

Brenda cut her off quickly. "Hey, there's no need to apologize around here for letting your feelings show. And Theresa, we all care about you."

"Do you think I'm wrong?" Theresa asked.

Brenda shook her head sharply. "It's not up to me to decide if you're right or wrong. My job is to help you find a way to adjust to your new life, and to feel better about yourself. Working things out at home is only part of it. The rest," Brenda added pointing to Theresa's heart, "is in there. You have to like yourself before you can like other people."

Not wanting to push Theresa too far all at once, Brenda stood. "Just think about what we've discussed."

"I will," Theresa promised wiping her eyes with her sleeve. "And thanks for the Coke."

"Anytime," Brenda told her with a smile. "And listen, if you need to talk, and Tony or I aren't around, call me at home. My number's in the office."

"I wouldn't want to bother you."

"I like to be bothered. And I won't forget about you, no matter how hard you try to make me. So call me if you need me!" Brenda ordered with mock sternness.

Theresa smiled again. "Okay, I promise."

Brenda turned and left the dorm room. The instant she reached the hallway, she looked around for Jake. Her anger was piqued and she wanted to give him a piece of her mind. He was nowhere in sight, however.

58

Typical, thought Brenda. But in spite of her anger, she was also disappointed that Jake had gone. From the moment she'd sensed his presence, her stomach had begun doing calisthenics. She was trembling now, and her face felt flushed and hot.

Why does he affect me like this? she asked herself. Halfway to the stairs, Brenda stopped. She leaned on the wall and shook her head back and forth. Don't run after him, she told herself. This is wrong.

What was wrong, though? What was it that she was feeling?

Willing her thoughts to stop tumbling madly, Brenda forced herself to think logically again. She stood in the hallway until her pounding heart had quieted and her emotions were under control.

Soon reality returned and with it, the everyday sounds of Garfield House. As she heard the buzzing and beeping of downstairs video games and snatches of conversation, she relaxed.

By the time Brenda had reached the first floor she had convinced herself that her feelings for Jake were not based on an attraction of any sort, but because he reminded her of the way she had been when she'd first arrived at Garfield House. His rebellious front was just an act to protect himself. Brenda was sure that deep down inside, Jake Hoover was a nice person. That side of him was just waiting to be discovered and set free.

"Brenda," Tony called from behind her. Turning, she waited for the head counselor to catch up. "How did it go with Theresa?"

Brenda smiled. "Not bad. I think I got her to open up more and see things a little differently — maybe."

"That's a good start. Have you seen Jake around?" Tony asked suddenly.

"I saw him upstairs a few minutes ago."

"Where?"

Brenda paused. "The second floor," she whispered.

"On the stairs?" Tony asked.

Brenda closed her eyes. "In the dorm."

"The dorm!" Tony shouted loud enough to make two of the kids doing hall clean-up duty stop to look at them. "What was he doing in the girls' dorm? That's it! This time he's gone too far!"

Seeing the rage on Tony's face, Brenda started forward in alarm. "Tony," she said, putting her hand on his arm, "he was probably just looking for someone."

"Not in the girls' dorm. He knows the rules even if he doesn't obey them."

Suddenly, Brenda remembered the strained look on Tony's face when he'd asked her earlier if she had seen Jake. A warning bell rang in her mind. "What . . . what's wrong?"

"As soon as I find him nothing will be wrong, because Jake Hoover will be history at Garfield House," Tony said angrily.

"What?"

"I've had it with him! I'm throwing him out!"

"No, you can't do that," Brenda pleaded.

"Oh no? Watch me," Tony said as he started toward the stairs.

Chapter
7

Brenda was frozen to the spot. Helplessly, she watched Tony's retreating back as he started up the stairs. Then all at once, something clicked in her mind, and Brenda knew what she had to do.

She couldn't let Tony throw Jake out. It wasn't right. That was what Garfield House was here for — to help kids like Jake. With that thought uppermost in her mind, Brenda broke free of her trance and raced after Tony. She caught him when he was halfway up to the second floor.

"Tony, wait, please. You can't do this just because you don't like him."

Tony turned to Brenda. A muscle ticked angrily in his cheek. He sat down at the top of the stairs, and patted the spot next to him. When Brenda was seated, he said, "Liking or disliking Jake has nothing to do with it."

Brenda tried to understand why Tony, who

could tolerate almost anybody, wanted to get rid of Jake. "Then why do you want him out?"

"Jake is an outlaw, plain and simple. What he did last night proved it." Tony pointed to a group of kids hanging out by the soda machine. "See those kids? They're here because they need us. They try to follow the rules because they want to stay, because they want to get help. Jake doesn't."

Tony paused to look at Brenda. It was difficult to read the expression on his face.

"Last night Jake came in after curfew. And because he's such a big man, he snuck in instead of signing in. He tripped the silent burglar alarm and we had two patrol cars here from midnight until one this morning."

"Oh no," Brenda whispered, already knowing what Tony would say next.

"Oh yes. We didn't need that. The people in the neighborhood aren't thrilled with us as it is. I know I'm going to hear about the sirens and flashing lights for a long time to come."

A terrible picture formed in Brenda's mind. It was Jake, looking tired and desperate and prowling the streets at night with nowhere to go. "You can't just give up on him, Tony," Brenda pleaded. "This is probably Jake's last chance. If you throw him out, he'll end up getting into some really bad trouble."

Tony studied her face intently. "What would you suggest?"

Taking a deep breath, Brenda burst out, "Let me try and work with him. Maybe I can get him to see what he's doing."

In the silence that followed her plea, Tony's brows knitted together and his mouth formed a tight line. Brenda held her breath, praying that he wouldn't say no.

"All right," Tony relented, finally. "I'll let you have a two-week probationary period. If Jake hasn't made any attempt to become part of Garfield House by then, he's out."

Brenda smiled wide, leaned over, and gave Tony a big kiss on his cheek. "Thank you, Tony, I won't let you down."

"I know that, kiddo," he said, giving her another of his famous bear hugs. "Just don't let yourself down."

Elated with Tony's decision, Brenda said, "I'll go tell him."

"No, I'll tell him. *After* I read him the riot act for last night, and for his being in the girls' dorm."

Brenda stayed on the steps long after Tony had gone, thinking about Jake Hoover, and how she would go about penetrating his tough exterior. "I'll do it," she promised herself. "I know he's worth it."

Two hours after her talk with Tony, Brenda was floating around Garfield House. Her main objective was to watch Jake Hoover, who seemed to have mastered the trick of doing nothing while nevertheless appearing busy.

Ever since she had convinced Tony not to kick Jake out of Garfield House, she had been watching Jake go from room to room. At one point he'd joined a group of boys who were talking about school, listened to them for a little while, and then moved on to something else. She noticed that he never took part in any of the conversations, and when someone did speak to him, his usual answer was a shrug or a glare.

She wondered if she was watching him too closely. Once, Jake had stopped in his tracks and turned to look at her. A secretive and shadowy smile had sprung onto his lips, and, embarrassed, Brenda had looked away.

What she learned confirmed two things. First, Jake was a complete loner and second, he was an expert at getting out of activities he didn't want to do. Since she'd begun watching Jake, Tony had asked for work volunteers three different times. The jobs were the sort of chores that all the kids who lived at Garfield House or who came there during the day for help were expected to do. But each time Tony had asked for help, Jake had melted into the background until Tony had found his volunteers.

She walked into the brightly-painted game room where a few kids stood around. Of the five video games that lined one wall — a gift from a vending company to Garfield House — two were in use. A knock hockey set dominated the center of the room, and was being put to a test by two furiously involved twelve-year-old boys.

The stereo was on. Springsteen's husky voice reached out to Brenda. Going over to an empty chair, she sat down heavily to think. As she did, the girl playing the second game turned around. It was Carla.

"How are you, Carla?" Brenda asked.

"Good. Things are starting to work out better at home."

"I'm glad to hear that."

Carla laughed. "Yeah, so am I." She looked at her watch and said, "I'd better get going. Tony asked my mother to come over today. He wants us to get together with him, and believe it or not, she's coming."

Brenda nodded encouragingly and waved goodbye to Carla, pleased that the girl's problems were starting to ease up. A meeting between her mother and Tony was a good sign. It meant that Carla was trying to accept her life at home.

But what about Jake? she asked herself. Leaning her head back, she closed her eyes. How can I get through to him? It was a question Brenda wasn't sure she could answer.

"Hey all you guys and gals out there in K-100 land, listen to this," came the brisk voice of Tommy Taylor, K-100's afternoon DJ. "Starting this Sunday morning, Teen Beat returns for another summer. So don't forget to tune in for your special show this Sunday at ten A.M. with DJ Monica Ford of Kennedy High."

Brenda smiled when she heard Monica's name. Talk about someone who had changed and gotten her act together! She remembered how shy Monica had been when she'd first met her. Everyone can change, she realized, even me, even Jake.

"Can I sit with you?"

Brenda's eyes popped open to find the object of her thoughts standing a few feet in front of her. The air in the game room was suddenly charged with electricity.

Once again Jake was wearing jeans and a T-shirt. The shirt was red today, and it stretched tightly across his chest. Her breath caught, and Brenda nodded. "Sure," she said, trying to ignore the way her heart had started beating quickly.

Jake came slowly to the couch, his walk graceful and catlike. He sat down next to Brenda and his eyes roamed across her face. "What were you smiling about?"

"Was I smiling?"

"You didn't look like you were in pain," he replied. Slowly, almost seductively, Jake smiled, showing a set of perfect white teeth.

"I was listening to the announcement about Sunday's Teen Beat show. A friend of mine is the DJ."

Jake raised his eyebrows. "Not bad.

"Listen," he said, lowering his voice, "I want to thank you for standing up to Tony for me. I don't know what I would have done if I'd had to leave here — this is the only place I have left to come to." With his last word, he put his hand on top of Brenda's.

His skin was warm where it touched hers. A thousand sparks danced across the top of her hand. Brenda looked into Jake's dark eyes, and felt strangely weak. Gently she withdrew her hand. "I thought it might be," she said in a controlled voice. "You're on probation, you know."

"Yeah, Tony made sure I knew that. He said that if it wasn't for you, I'd already be gone."

"That was a stupid thing you did last night," Brenda told him.

Jake gave a strange laugh and looked away. When he turned back, his expression was grim. "Yeah, I'm famous for doing stupid things."

Was he putting himself down, or was he really bragging? Brenda wondered. She decided to be firm with him. "Don't do any more stupid things, because I'm responsible for you now." The instant she spoke, she realized her mistake. Jake's eyes flickered dangerously. He smiled again, but his grin reminded Brenda of a cat ready to pounce. His eyes were locked tightly on hers. "Yes ma'am," Jake drawled. Then he gave a little salute.

"I'm being serious," she said.

"So am I," Jake whispered in a husky voice.

Brenda was mesmerized. Jake's physical presence was so powerful, she felt as if he were a magnet and she a tiny scrap of metal being drawn to him.

"Jake," Brenda said, shaking her head to break the tension, "Garfield House is important to the kids here. It's important to me, and I hope it's important to you, as well. Is it, Jake?"

Jake's eyes became hooded. He stared across the room, looking out the window. "It's home right now, so I guess it is important."

Brenda studied Jake's profile. His strong jaw jutted out stubbornly, and his dark unruly hair served only to emphasize his good looks. If only he would let her help him!

Shaking her head, Brenda stood up. "We're

working together next week. I'll see you Monday morning, right?"

Jake winked at her. "Okay."

Brenda smiled as she left him, but she wondered deep inside if it really was okay. Could she help Jake find what he needed, or this time had she gotten in over her head?

Brad took off his white orderly jacket and sat down on the couch. Picking up his plastic coffee cup, he held it between trembling palms. He stared at his coffee in fascination, watching the way the liquid rippled in response to the shaking of his hands.

Never before in his life had Brad been so totally exhausted. He was so tired that all he wanted to do was lie down and sleep. But he couldn't lie down, he reminded himself, because that would require more time than his fifteen-minute break.

Looking outside at the bright day, he sighed and felt the empty spot in his heart grow larger. "I'm sorry," he whispered to Brenda's image, knowing that he had not handled his phone call to her in the right way.

Brad had never liked breaking his promise, but this time he hadn't been able to help it. They were so shorthanded that the hospital had been like a zoo. The bus accident earlier that morning hadn't helped matters — thirty-eight people had been hurt.

Two emergency room doctors had drafted Brad to help them move the victims of the bus accident around and to comfort them whenever he could. He had spent the first three and a half hours of his work shift running between the patients. When everything had calmed down, he and one of the regular orderlies had been assigned to move the new patients to their rooms. That had taken another hour.

Finally, Brad had been given a fifteen-minute break, which was the reason he was now in the lounge, thinking about Brenda and how he had messed things up that morning. It wasn't until Brenda had hung up on him that he realized he had made a mistake. He should have been more subtle and apologetic when he'd canceled their date. But he hadn't been, and now it was too late.

"But it isn't!" Brad told himself aloud. Suddenly he wanted to apologize to Brenda for being so inconsiderate. Standing, Brad went to the pay phone and dialed the Austin's number. He let the phone ring several times and, just as he was about to hang up, Chris answered the phone.

"Is Brenda there?" he asked.

"Why?" Chris asked in a peevish voice that was most unlike her usual self.

"Are you mad at something?" Brad asked.

"Yes I am, Brad. I'm mad at you," came the reply.

"At me? What did I do to you?" Brad asked, confused and hurt. There was a pause. "Chris?"

"Sometimes you're really dense," Chris informed him in a gentler voice. "I'm upset with you for breaking your date with Brenda. Brad, she was counting on you."

"I know, but I couldn't help it. They had an

emergency here and they needed me. Besides, Brenda understands."

"Sure she does. But if you keep on breaking your dates, she won't understand much longer."

"That's why I'm calling," Brad explained. "I want to make it up to her."

"Brad, I'm glad to hear that, but the only way you can make it up to her is by *being* with her instead of at the hospital."

"Is that what she said?" Brad asked, surprised that Brenda would say that when she knew it wasn't his fault for breaking their date.

"No," Chris admitted. "That's what I said."

"I see." Brad's grip on the phone tightened. He closed his eyes and took a deep breath. "Is Brenda there?" he asked, feeling a little angry.

"She went to Garfield House after *you* canceled the picnic. She hasn't come back yet."

"Would you tell her that I called?"

Chris sighed. "You know I will."

"Chris, they really needed me at the hospital today," Brad said, trying to explain, "and I learned a lot." His voice brightened. "Especially about emergency room medicine."

"I'm glad the job is helping you. But, I've got to go now, Ted's waiting for me." Brad started to say good-bye when Chris interrupted him. "Hold on, I think Brenda just got home."

A few seconds later, Brenda's throaty voice came through the telephone line.

Brad felt a rush of warmth when he heard her voice. "Hi," he said quickly. "I called to apologize for today. I feel rotten about what happened."

"Good. So do I," Brenda admitted.

"Bren, I'd like to see you tonight." When she didn't speak, Brad pushed on. "Can I came over later? We can go for a ride, or do whatever you'd like to do. I really want to see you."

"Won't you be too tired?" Brenda finally asked.

Brad's breath came out like a long sigh. "Not for you. I miss you. I miss you a lot."

"Oh Brad, I — I miss you, too, and I'd like to see you tonight."

"I'll be by after work," he promised, smiling at the receiver as he hung up.

He went back to the couch and sat down again. His hands no longer shook, and he felt ready to face the world again. Brad breathed a sigh of relief. Brenda wasn't angry with him; he had been right all along to believe that she understood what this summer meant to him. That was why Brenda was so special. She'd always understand, even when other girls wouldn't.

"Brad Davidson to the second floor," came a woman's voice from the overhead speaker.

Groaning, Brad stood up. "Duty calls," he muttered, but he liked the way his name had sounded over the P.A. system. He liked it a lot.

Chapter
8

"What am I going to do?"

"You're not going to panic," Kim commanded Monica, who acted as if she had to face a firing squad on Sunday instead of an eager audience.

The trouble was, K-100 had moved the show's starting day up a week. Instead of the first Teen Beat show being aired a week from Sunday, the first show would be this Sunday.

"Why shouldn't I panic?" Monica asked, her face tense and pinched with nervousness. "I'm not ready yet. I was supposed to have another week."

Kim looked up at the cloudless night sky. She wished Monica would relax for a little while and joke around the way she used to. It was such a lovely evening; the stars were shining brightly, and the quarter moon looked as if it had been painted on black velvet. The two girls were walking to Kim's house, and although it wasn't very late, the street was quiet.

"It's too nice a night to worry. Everything will work out."

Monica windmilled her arms in the air. "That's easy for you to say. You don't have to make a fool out of yourself in front of a million kids!"

"You won't be in front of a million kids. You'll be by yourself in a cozy radio station," Kim informed her with perfect logic.

"It's the same thing! What am I going to do?" Monica wailed again.

"You're going to stop driving me crazy. That's what!" Kim declared. She put a comforting arm around her friend. "Listen, why don't we just stop worrying about Sunday and go over to my place and wait for the guys. We're going bowling tonight, remember? And you deserve to have some fun."

"I should never have done it," Monica said as she stared up at a street lamp.

"I'll make chocolate brownies — they're your favorite. Remember?" Kim tempted.

"It was a mistake," continued Monica, oblivious to the offer.

"What was a mistake?" Kim asked, exasperated.

"Sending in that tape." On her last word, Monica stopped dead in her tracks.

"I don't understand," Kim said.

Monica stared at Kim, a look of desperation in her eyes. "I can't go bowling. I have to work on the show."

"You mean you're not going to come tonight?" Kim asked, shaking her head in disbelief.

Monica glanced away. When she looked back, Kim saw the open plea for understanding in

73

Monica's eyes. "I'm sorry, Kim," Monica faltered. "I really am, but you're my best friend. You just have to understand."

"I'm trying to, Monica," Kim replied, wishing she could shake some sense into her friend. "It's just that since you've become the DJ for Teen Beat, all you do is work on your show. And I don't think taking one night off will hurt you."

Monica stiffened. "I have to work on the show!" she pleaded. She turned and started back to her house, calling over her shoulder. "Please Kim, tell Peter for me, please. He knows what I'm going through."

"I wonder if you know what *he's* going through," Kim whispered to Monica's retreating back.

With a shrug of helplessness, Kim started off again. Five minutes later, she was at her house. Peter's Volkswagen beetle was already parked in her driveway. Inside Woody and Peter were listening to the stereo in the family room, and her mother was in the kitchen, testing a new recipe.

When she entered the paneled family room, both boys' heads turned. "Hi guys," Kim said with more cheerfulness than she felt.

"Where's Monica?" Peter asked while Woody kissed her lightly on the cheek.

Kim closed her eyes for a second, relishing the gentleness of Woody's lips before facing Peter. "Uh — well — she's not coming tonight. She's worried about her show. She thought she'd have another week to get it ready. . . ."

Kim saw a flash of pain cloud Peter's eyes. His smile disappeared, and a frown took its place. "She's already had a week," he muttered in a low voice. "This is getting crazy!"

Kim was torn between her two friends; she sympathized with Peter, but she also knew what Monica was going through. The last thing she wanted to do was to take sides. But she had to try to explain Monica's position — for both their sakes. "She's just worried. She doesn't want to let anyone down."

"Oh yeah? What about me?" Peter retorted angrily.

"Especially you, Peter," Kim said in a gentle voice. "She wants you to be proud of her."

"Hey," Woody chimed in, snapping his repaired red suspenders comically, "let's go bowling and forget about everything else."

Peter shook his head. "You two go ahead. I need to get some air and clear out my head."

"C'mon, Peter," Woody said, putting his hand on his friend's shoulder. "Don't let this get you down. She does want you to be proud of her."

Peter stepped back, dislodging Woody's hand. "Doesn't anyone understand?" he asked, looking from Kim to Woody and back to Kim again. His eyes were open wide, his hands were held out in a gesture of frustration. "She doesn't have to prove herself to me. I'm already proud of her!"

"Peter," Kim began, but Peter shook his head and sidestepped his friends. "I have to get outside," he insisted. "Good-night."

When he was gone, Kim turned to Woody. "I feel so bad for both of them. Hold me," she whispered, moving closer to Woody.

Woody drew her into his arms and held her

75

tightly. He kissed the top of her head, and Kim felt a rush of love for him. She was so lucky; there was no doubt in her mind that Woody would always be there for her. Drawing back just a little, she gazed into his eyes. "I love you."

Woody smiled and kissed her. Their lips met gently, and the warmth of his touch lingered on long after the kiss had ended.

"I hate seeing Peter like this," Woody said when he released Kim.

"Then we have to do something to set things right," Kim ventured.

Kim was thoughtful for a moment. Then an idea came to her. "How about a celebration party on Sunday night? We can get the whole gang together and make it a surprise party! No one will tell Monica or Peter."

"Uh-uh," Woody warned. "You've got to tell Peter."

"Why?"

"Because he's upset enough not to want to go to a party for Monica. And I think he's jealous, too."

"That's pretty obvious," Kim agreed. "The only person who doesn't realize that is Monica."

"Leave Peter to me," Woody stated with a big smile. "I'll work something out."

Kim stepped closer to Woody again. She looked into his warm brown eyes and said, "I know you will."

Woody bent down again to kiss Kim. Just as his arms went around her, and Kim felt herself melting, a low cough came from behind them.

Pushing Kim away so quickly that she almost

fell down, Woody turned to face Mrs. Barrie. His face was beet red.

"Don't look so guilty," Mrs. Barrie reassured them. "You're not doing anything I didn't."

Before Woody could recover enough to reply, Kim spoke up, ignoring the flush on her cheeks that was a combination of the emotion of their kiss and embarrassment of being caught by surprise. "Mom, I know you and Dad are going out Sunday night. Could I have a few of the kids over?"

"Hmmm, what's a few?" Mrs. Barrie asked, suspiciously.

"Just some of the gang. Brenda and Brad, Chris and Ted, Woody, Phoebe, Michael, Sasha. . . ."

"Well . . ." Mrs. Barrie considered, biting her lower lip, "as long as you keep the guest list down. But, what about Monica? I didn't hear her name. Where are Peter and Monica by the way?" she asked, glancing around the family room. "I thought they were going out with you two?"

"They were, but Monica had to work on her show tonight," Kim explained. "Mom, that's what the party is all about. It's a surprise party to celebrate Monica's first show. She's been under a lot of tension and stress and has been working really hard — I think a little party would be wonderful for her."

Mrs. Barrie nodded. "I guess it'll be all right. But I don't want my kitchen destroyed. We've got a luncheon to cater on Monday. Understood?"

"Understood!" Kim and Woody said at the same time.

Before Mrs. Barrie was halfway out of the family room, Woody pulled Kim down beside him on the floor.

"This had better work," he said.

"It will. It has to," Kim replied, giggling. "I don't want Monica's job to break them up. Now," she added, as the familiar excitement of cooking for a party began to build, "what should I serve?"

"Hold on! This is just a casual party, not a catered affair," Woody protested, obviously thinking of all the work that might be involved.

"Why can't it be both? After all, I am in the catering business."

Woody smiled. His eyes twinkled. "Okay. How about catering to me?"

"Maybe I will," Kim teased, lowering her eyelids and gazing up at him. "After we make some phone calls and decide what we're going to serve," she added quickly.

"Spoilsport!" Woody cried with a fake pout as he leaned toward her and tried to catch her in his arms.

Laughing, Kim neatly dodged his arms, and rose gracefully to her feet. "First things first!" she commanded sternly before kissing Woody on the top of his head and then racing over to the phone.

"That sounds great, Kim. I'll tell the others." After hanging up, Chris turned to survey the small group camped out in the Austin's den.

Ted was lying across the leather couch. Phoebe Hall and her friend, Michael Rifkin, were sitting on the floor going over the Austin's classical record collection. Brad and Brenda were sitting near them, holding hands quietly.

They had all gotten together to watch a movie that Ted had rented. It was *The Day of the Triffids,* a classic science-fiction movie. But they had yet to put the movie on, because everyone had been so busy talking about their summer activities and making future plans.

Chris was thrilled with her job in Congressman Barnes's office and had found the political scene every bit as fascinating as she had hoped.

Most of the gang were also having a good time, and Chris noted with interest that Phoebe's eyes lit up and her voice became especially animated when she talked about the few things she and Michael were doing together, and about the extra voice lessons that his mother was giving her. But when Chris glanced over at Brad and Brenda, she realized they'd said next to nothing all night.

"Hey world!" she shouted, moving to the center of the room and placing her hands on her hips. When she had everyone's attention, she made her announcement. "Party time! Kim Barrie called to say that she and Woody are planning a surprise party to celebrate Monica's first show on K-100! At the Barries.' "

Phoebe looked up from the album jacket Michael held. "What a great idea! When is it?"

"This Sunday night," Chris announced happily. The party would be the first real one of the summer. The next bash wasn't planned until July Fourth, still a couple of weeks away.

"All right!" Ted shouted, swiveling gracefully

on the couch until he was sitting up. "If it's at the Barries', that means good food."

"But remember it's a surprise party," Chris admonished. "No one tells Monica."

"Can everyone make it? Michael?" Chris asked.

Michael looked shyly from Chris to Phoebe. "No problem," he said when he met Phoebe's eyes.

"Great," Chris declared before turning her gaze to Brad, who seemed half asleep. "Brad?" she asked.

"I'm not sure," Brad admitted, opening his eyes wide and glancing at Brenda. "I've got to work the eleven to seven shift on Sunday."

Chris's breath caught when she saw Brenda's eyes roll upward. "The party's set for eight-thirty," Chris informed him.

"It's a long day. And I work pretty hard."

"Listen to him," Brenda said at last. "This is the first party of the summer, and Brad's last summer at home before college. Can you believe all he thinks about is work!" Brenda shook her head sadly.

"I didn't say I wouldn't go," Brad replied defensively.

"You didn't say you would go either," Brenda flung back as she stood and marched out of the den.

Chris stared at her stepsister's rigid back and longed to be able to help her. "I can't believe you're that insensitive," she whispered to Brad as she started after Brenda.

Before she moved two steps, her arm was

80

caught from behind. Turning, she found herself staring into Brad's eyes.

"Wait, Chris, please," he asked.

Chris stared at him, surprised that he had stopped her and aware that everyone in the room was watching.

"Maybe you're right, Chris," Brad said in a low voice. "Maybe I have been taking things for granted. Stay here and let me try to talk with Brenda."

Chris smiled at Brad and slowly exhaled. "That sounds like a good idea."

Brenda stormed through the brightly lit hallway and stepped into the kitchen. Her mind was spinning and her anger made her feel as if she couldn't breathe. No matter where she turned, the walls seemed to be closing in.

When she heard footsteps coming from behind her, she had only one thought — escape. Without waiting to see who it was, Brenda half ran past the long butcher block counter toward the kitchen door and the backyard.

Opening the door, she heard Brad call out her name, but did not stop. Outside, the night was alive with sounds. Crickets called, and night birds sang beneath the light of the moon. A moment later, Brad was running up behind her.

"Will you please wait a minute?" he called.

Brenda shook her head and kept walking, but Brad grabbed her arm and stopped her.

"I've been wrong," Brad pleaded, forcing her to look at him. "I've been thinking about myself and not about you. And I don't want to lose you because I've been stupid."

Brenda's breath caught. Looking at Brad, standing so handsome and tall in the moonlight, she knew that she loved him. From behind them came the music that introduced the movie. She didn't move, though. Seeing the film didn't matter, being with Brad did.

As if he had read her thoughts, Brad pulled her gently into his arms. Brenda's throat tightened with emotion when he began stroking her hair.

"I love you, Brenda," he whispered, kissing her forehead reverently, as if she were a precious jewel.

Brenda smiled as the warmth of his body, and the sound of his words mingled with her senses. "I love you, too, Brad," she told him. "Do you remember the last time we were out here at night?"

Brad's eyes brightened. He looked around the back yard. "After my graduation. We spent the whole night sitting and talking."

Brenda slipped from his embrace, but quickly caught his hand in hers. Kneeling, she drew him down to the grass with her. After they were seated next to each other, she squeezed his hand and spoke. "We made plans, Brad," she reminded him. "Plans to do things together. Can we try, really try to make this summer a good one?"

"Yes," he promised, reaching out to caress her cheek.

Brenda covered his hand with hers, and pressed it tightly to her skin. "I do love you, Brad," she whispered before releasing his hand and going back into his arms.

Chapter
9

Brenda leaned her head on the back of the seat. Moonlight and street lamps flickered across the windshield of Brad's silver Honda as he drove carefully along the avenue.

Slowly, Brenda lifted Brad's hand to her lips and gently caressed his skin for several long, delicious seconds.

From the corner of her eye, she saw Brad glance at her. A smile again brightened his face and his eyes glowed.

A chill raced down Brenda's back. "Careful," she warned Brad in her huskiest voice, "you're driving."

"No," he said with a quick shake of his head. "*You're* driving . . . me crazy!"

"That's my job, isn't it?" Brenda asked, using her throatiness to tease him even more.

"To drive me crazy?"

"If I have to drive you crazy to pay attention

to me, then that's what I'll do," she declared in a stronger voice than she had meant.

"I do pay attention to you, Brenda," Brad said in a thoughtful way as Brenda lowered their hands to her lap.

"Sometimes," Brenda added. "It just seems that most of the time we're together, all we talk about is your job."

"I get carried away," he told her. "But I'm trying to get better. How about trying something different?" he asked.

"Okay. What?"

"Tell me about what's happening at Garfield House," Brad suggested.

Surprised and pleased, Brenda began enthusiastically, "I was assigned a really hard case. Tony wanted to throw him out of the house, but I talked Tony into letting me try to work with him. He's a guy who makes no attempt to fit in with the other kids. He's — "

"Boy, talk about hard cases." Brad cut her off suddenly. "You should have seen the guy who came in today. He was having an allergic reaction to some medication and it was making him act crazy. He was fighting everyone. It took three of us to hold him down so that the doctor could give him an injection."

"Stop!" Brenda shouted at the top of her voice. Immediately Brad yanked his hand from hers and hit the brakes.

"What?" he asked looking quickly around.

"Not the car — *you*! I'm supposed to be telling you about Garfield House, and *you're* supposed to be listening," she stated bluntly.

Brad grimaced. "I did it again, didn't I?" he asked, turning to look at her with a little-boy-caught-in-the-cookie-jar expression.

"You sure did," Brenda told him.

"Bren, I'm sorry," Brad whispered. "Listen, tell me about this guy you're trying to help."

Brenda saw the large green sign for the Rose Hill exit coming up and, sighing, she shook her head. "We're almost home and it's a long story. We'll talk about it another time, okay?"

When Brad pulled to a stop in the Austin driveway a little while later, he unhooked his seatbelt and leaned over to her.

Before Brenda could say anything, he unhooked her belt and drew her to him, kissing her deeply. When the kiss ended, Brenda drew back to look at Brad.

"I'll see you tomorrow night," she said.

"Count on it," Brad told her.

Brenda turned to stare at Brad. "I am," she said, her voice filled with new meaning.

Chapter 10

Brenda looked around at the group that had taken over the Austin den to listen to Monica's show. Chris and Ted were holding hands as usual, Phoebe was half lying across a bolster she'd stolen from the sofa, while Sasha reclined next to her, a note pad in her hand and thoughtful look on her face. It was the regular crowd, she noted, so why did she feel so different, so out of it?

Peter had shown up with Woody twenty minutes earlier, and told everyone that Kim decided to stay home so that she could get a head start on her baking.

"All right you guys," Woody yelled. "Let's pay attention now. That means you, too, Brenda," he added pointedly.

Before Brenda had a chance for a comeback, Ted spoke up. "Woody, what happened to your red suspenders? They finally die of the plague?"

Woody slipped his thumbs into the shiny, new

yellow suspenders holding up his baggy khaki pants and comically tugged at them. "It's Sunday, Mason. Even red suspenders have to have a day off."

"It's about time," Phoebe said with a smile.

"Too bad Brad can't do the same," Brenda commented without looking at anyone.

"Two minutes," Peter called without taking his eyes from the radio.

"It's not a TV," Ted joked, "you don't have to watch it to hear Monica."

"Enough, Mason!" Woody shouted loudly enough to snap Brenda out of her lethargy. She looked up just as Chris's hand covered Ted's mouth. At that very instant, Monica Ford's voice issued from the two three-foot hi-tech speakers on each side of the stereo.

"Good morning, and welcome to Teen Beat. I'm Monica Ford, your summer DJ, and this is the 'Boss'!" Monica announced. Before the *s* of "boss" was gone, the first notes of Springsteen's classic "Born To Run" were smoothly pounding out.

"All right!" Woody shouted. 'Way to go!"

Even Brenda smiled. But, her smile faltered when she saw the strained look on Peter's face. She wondered what was bothering him. Maybe the same thing that's bothering me, Brenda thought. Whatever that is.

"What do you think?" Suddenly Brenda realized Peter had asked her a question.

Embarrassed because she hadn't been paying attention to Monica's show, Brenda shrugged self-consciously. "Good. Like you."

"Thanks," Peter said. "You seem a little low this morning. Are you okay?"

"I'm fine," Brenda replied automatically.

"You don't look fine. I mean you always look good but. . . ."

Brenda laughed softly before shaking her head. "It's nothing. I was just thinking about the way Brad's been talking about his job."

"I know what you mean," Peter said in a low voice before he turned back to stare at the radio.

Brenda picked up on the downbeat tone of his words. She remembered Chris telling her that one of the reasons for Monica's party was because Peter and Monica were having problems.

Brenda sensed that Peter's problem was Monica's job. Stupid! she told herself. Of course that's what's wrong. Everyone knew that Peter had wanted a job at a radio station this summer more than anything else.

Shifting her gaze, Brenda watched Phoebe divide her attention between the small needlepoint she was working on and Sasha, who was scribbling notes. "Sash," Brenda called, "Is that for next year's paper?"

Sasha looked up, brushing her long dark hair out of her eyes. "I thought I'd do an article about summer jobs for the first issue of *The Red and The Gold*," she explained before bending down to her task.

"Good segue," Peter said, commenting on Monica's latest remarks coming from the radio.

Brenda liked the proud look on his face. "She is doing a good job isn't she?"

Peter smiled. "Yeah," he said.

"Peter, I understand how hard it can be when someone gets a little distant because of work," she said in a voice that only he could hear. "If you need to talk, I'm always available to listen."

Peter gazed at her and slowly nodded his head. "Thanks, Brenda, I appreciate the offer." As they looked at each other, Monica announced that she would be back after a commercial.

Peter glanced at his watch. "The show's over, she's just going to make her closing announcements," he informed the group.

"Great show!" Woody cried. "All right Monica!"

"She was good, Peter, really good," Chris said.

"Wow," Phoebe added, "was that our shy little Monica Ford?"

"Wait," Chris cried, "she's back on."

Everyone quieted as Monica started to make her closing announcement. Brenda knew what was coming, and a ripple of nervousness raced along her spine.

"In two weeks," Monica told her audience, "our special guest will be Brenda Austin, who will talk about Garfield House. Garfield is the halfway house where any of you can go for counseling and to get help if you have problems at home."

"When did that happen?" Ted asked from behind her.

"Yesterday," Chris answered proudly. "Monica called to ask if Brenda would do a guest interview. And we all know how Brenda feels about Garfield House."

"I think that's great," Sasha broke in. "What are you going to talk about?"

Brenda shrugged. "I figured I'd let Monica do the interviewing. It's her show."

"What's her show?" came Brad's voice.

Brenda whipped around in disbelief to find her boyfriend standing in the den. She stared at him for several seconds, just to make sure it wasn't a fantasy. After she blinked her eyes and Brad was still there, she glanced around the room and saw that everyone else was looking at Brad as if he were a ghost.

"I didn't think my effect on you guys was that awesome," Brad joked.

Phoebe was the first to recover. "What happened, did they close the hospital?"

"Very funny. No, they changed my shift again and I got the day off," he explained. "Which is why I'm here. I want to see my favorite lady in the whole world."

"Oh, Brad," Brenda whispered as she stood and went over to him.

Just as Brenda reached Brad, Woody got up from the chair and said, "Speaking of eating. . . ."

"Who's speaking of eating?" Ted asked his friend as he helped Chris to her feet.

"No one yet, but we all will be soon. It's time to get over to Kim's."

Brad looked at Brenda. "I was thinking about Rosemont Park," he whispered.

"After we help Kim, okay?" When Brad nodded, Brenda squeezed his hand. "I'm really glad you came over."

"Me, too."

* * *

At exactly nine-fifteen, Peter turned his car onto Willow Court and headed for Kim's house.

"I didn't know Kim and Woody were going to the movies with us," Monica said when she realized where Peter was taking her.

"Woody wasn't sure," Peter remarked casually, "so I told him we'd come by just in case. All right?"

"Sure," Monica replied, smiling at Peter. "I did okay today, didn't I?" she asked for the umpteenth time.

"Nah," Peter teased, but Monica hurried on, as if she hadn't heard him.

"I could have handled that third commercial lead-in a little better. Hank said I did fine," Monica explained, thinking about her engineer on the Teen Beat show, Hank Thompson. Hank had been a tremendous help — open, warm, and very encouraging.

"Speaking of Hank, how old is this electronic wizard?" Peter asked, his eyes narrowed in comic suspicion.

Monica laughed and reached across to pat Peter's hand. "He's ancient — at least thirty. And he's married. He brought his son in today; Marc is five, and he's really cute."

Peter slowed when he neared Kim's house, and then pulled smoothly into the driveway. "Let's go," he said to Monica after shutting off the engine.

"Why don't I wait here?" Monica offered. "It'll save time. The movie starts in a half hour. We'll barely make it."

"Come on in anyway," he urged. "I mean, if they're not going I'm sure they'll want to tell you how much they loved your show."

"It wasn't that great," Monica replied, but Peter's words made her feel good. "Okay."

They walked up to the house together, and Peter rang the bell. No one answered. "They must be in the family room," Peter said as he tried the doorknob.

The door swung open easily. There was a light on in the hall. "Let's go," he ordered, taking Monica's arm and leading her inside.

"We should wait, Peter," Monica protested as she was dragged along the hallway. "This isn't our house."

When they reached the family room, the lights were out. "They're not here," Monica said, unable to see anything inside the darkened room. "We'd better get going."

"They're here somewhere."

Monica started to shake her head, then froze as the lights suddenly flared on, and her ears were filled with noise.

"Surprise!" shouted everyone, popping up from behind the furniture.

Monica blinked madly, trying to clear the dancing orange flashes from her eyes. When she could see again, she found all her friends standing in the family room. Above their heads was a large paper banner that read: MONICA FORD, SUPERSTAR. A half dozen gaily colored balloons hung from beneath the banner.

"Oh, wow," Monica whispered. "I — " But she couldn't say another word, because a giant lump had grown inside her throat. She felt her eyes brimming with tears. Deeply touched, she turned to Peter. Gazing into his deep green eyes, she gave him a look of gratitude and love.

"Congratulations. You were great today," Sasha told Monica as she rushed over and gave her a kiss on her cheek.

"Terrific," Chris added, kissing Monica's other cheek. "We're all proud of you."

"Say something," Kim cried.

Monica turned to Kim, her vision blurred. "I — you guys are the best!"

"Awwwright!" Ted shouted. "Let's get this party going. Food!" he cried, turning and heading to the long table draped with a white tablecloth.

The folding table that Kim's mother used for her catering business was filled with platters of food. In the center, a large silver tray was filled with cold cuts and cheese. Spreading out from the tray were platters of white bread, whole wheat, and rye. There was an enormous basket of fruit, and at each end of the table the dessert trays were heaped with the special Barrie pastries and cookies. The back of the table, where it touched the wall, was lined with cans of soda. Two white ice buckets were filled to overflowing.

"Wow," Monica said as she looked at the food table. "Kim, you really outdid yourself."

"Nothing's too good for my friend," Kim responded, proudly. "C'mon, dig in."

But Monica couldn't eat. All she wanted to do was look around at her friends' smiling faces. This surprise party meant more to her than anything she could think of. She wanted to laugh and cry and shout and dance all at once. How could she ever thank her friends — and Peter — enough?

A half hour after he'd brought the guest of honor to the party, Peter went over to the stereo to relieve Woody. He put on a Culture Club album and then turned back to watch what was happening. He tried to smile at everyone, while telling himself that this was Monica's night, not his. Above all, he knew that he must not let Monica, or anyone else know how he felt.

But when he looked at his girl friend — the professional radio DJ superstar — and saw the way her normally pale complexion was flushed with pleasure, he felt even worse.

"C'mon Peter," Brad called from a few feet away. "Let's have something to dance to, not whine to. Boy George just doesn't make it!"

"What do you want, *Doctor* Davidson? Frank Sinatra?" Peter responded sarcastically.

Brad shrugged and looked at Brenda. "What's wrong with him?"

Brenda guided Brad away from Peter, and over to the food table. She picked up a strawberry tart and handed it to Brad. "I think Peter's a little annoyed at all the fuss about Monica."

"Why should he be?" Brad asked. "Monica worked hard to get that job. And she's good. He should be happy for her."

"He is. He just needs time to adjust to it."

"Right," Brad replied, taking a bite of the tart. "Wow, this is good."

"Thanks," Kim laughed, coming up from behind Brad.

"I didn't see any of these this afternoon when we were setting up for the party," Brad told Kim.

"I didn't think you saw anything except Brenda," Kim quipped. "You two couldn't wait to get out of here."

"We had important things to discuss," Brad replied in a lofty tone, but his eyes were sparkling.

"I'll bet." When Kim glanced at Brenda, she saw her friend blush. "I love your top," Kim said, reaching out to touch the silken lace collar of Brenda's stark white tuxedo shirt. "And the bow tie is just perfect."

"Thanks, my stepfather loaned it to me," Brenda replied with a smile before turning to Brad and slipping her arm through his. "Let's dance," she suggested, and guided him to the middle of the room, where Phoebe and Michael were swaying to the music.

While Brenda rested her head on Brad's chest, enjoying the way his arms held her, she glanced at Peter. He was sitting by himself in front of the stereo.

Across the room, Monica was holding court. Sasha, wearing a lively print wrap around skirt, a lavender tank top, and open-toed sandals, was on Monica's left. On Monica's right, Kim, dressed in baggy white shorts and a hot-pink halter top, stood with her arm around Woody's waist.

When the song ended, Brenda glanced up at Brad. Just as she was about to say something, a sudden silence fell on the group as Laurie Ben- in the direction of the doorway as Laurie Bennington and Dick Westergard walked into the room.

Brenda stared at the couple in unfeigned surprise as Laurie paraded across the room in a brand-new designer dress, and swept Monica into an uncharacteristic embrace.

"You were wonderful," Laurie told her. "Really good. You showed up that guy from Carlton, who thought he was the greatest DJ in the world."

"Th-thanks," Monica stammered. She wasn't the only one who still had to get used to Laurie Bennington's new personality. Ever since the student council election race ended and she'd begun dating Dick Westergard, Laurie had become a different person, or so it seemed.

Still holding Brenda's hand, Brad walked over to Dick. "How's it going?"

"Good. Listen, Brad, thanks for those notes. I really appreciate it. It'll help me next year on the student council."

"Just make sure you work with Chris as a team. That's the only way you'll get anything done."

Dick nodded. "We'll get things done," he promised.

"Booooring," Brenda declared flirtatiously. "This is the summer. No school talk or politics. It's party time."

"Politics?" Chris inquired with a smile.

"Uh-oh, it's Congressman Barnes's special assistant, the honorable Chris Austin," Woody chimed in.

Chris pouted at Woody and nudged Ted.

"What?" Ted asked, licking the last of a blueberry tart from his mouth.

"Defend me," Chris pleaded.

"Awright you guys," Ted shouted, puffing his chest out and leering around the room, "anybody else makes a comment about Chris and they have to face me!"

"A fate worse than algebra," Sasha quipped, laughing at the antics in the middle of the room as the tension created by Laurie's entrance eased. "Peter, Monica worked hard today. How about helping us out in the record department? Music, maestro!"

Peter stared testily at Sasha. He didn't say anything; instead, he put on the Clash, and raised the volume until the walls vibrated.

Kim raced over to the stereo and lowered the noise level. "My dad will kill me if we blow a speaker."

"Sorry," Peter grumbled.

Kim started away but stopped. Reaching out, she put her hand on Peter's shoulder. "I know things aren't going the way you want them to. . . . But I think everything will be okay once Monica settles down. In the meantime, try and be happy for her."

"I'm trying Kim. I really am," Peter said, reaching for another album.

In the next couple of hours, the party continued in full swing.

Brenda kept Brad dancing alone with her for almost an hour. When he finally protested that he was about to pass out, she relented. Glancing at the open sliding glass door of the family room, she suggested that they go outside for some air.

Once outside, they walked across the grass, the sounds of the party fading quickly behind them. A cool breeze fluttered over them, tugging at Brenda's hair. Her hand was secured in Brad's warm grip. When she looked up at him, he was smiling. The moonlight accented the chip in his front tooth.

"Do you know that this is the first whole day since school ended that we've spent together?" Brenda said shyly.

Brad looked surprised. "Really?"

"Really! Thank you, Brad, I — I was about to give up," Brenda admitted.

"Give up on what?"

Brenda looked deeply into his eyes. "Us. You."

Brad squeezed her hand, and then let it go. He looked up at the stars. "Sometimes I get carried away with myself," he admitted.

"I know."

"Forgive me?"

"Of course I forgive you. But, you'll have to make it up to me," she teased.

"Punishment? All right, whatever I have to do, I'll do," he said in a hangdog voice.

"Good! Dinner a week from Saturday night. My folks are going to a dinner party at a friend's house that night. So, I'm cooking; you're eating. And you'd better not have to work!" Brenda warned him.

Brad scrunched his eyes shut for a second, pretending to consider the invitation. "I guess I can make it," he drawled. Then he gave Brenda a dazzling smile. "I work next Saturday, which means I'm off the Saturday after. No matter what, I promise I'll be there."

Brenda's heart felt lighter than it had in a long time. A sense of happiness swept over her. "Thank you, Brad," she whispered before rising onto her toes and offering him her lips.

The kiss she gave Brad, was more than just a kiss; it was the hope that perhaps everything would be all right.

Chapter
11

For Brenda, the first three days of the week flew by in a blur of action. On Wednesday afternoon at Garfield House her spirits were high. Tomorrow night, Thursday, she had a date with Brad. They would be doubling with Peter and Monica. Monica had gotten tickets to the Wolftrap amphitheater, and had invited Brenda and Brad because she knew how much Brad liked the Beethoven sonatas.

Back to the problem at hand, Brenda ordered herself. Listening to the discussion with half an ear, she looked around the blue walls of the group session room of Garfield House. Her eyes flicked to Jake Hoover, who was sitting across from her, watching the boy on his left speak. In profile, his features looked especially striking.

Brenda tried to focus her attention on the boy who was speaking, but her thoughts stubbornly continued to wander. Since Monday morning, she had been devoting most of her time at Garfield House to Jake Hoover. Jake, however, had spent all of his time trying to avoid working with Brenda. Even though they'd been spending time together, she had not been able to get Jake to open up at all. Brenda knew she had to change that soon, or she would have to give up on him.

But I can't do that! was her immediate thought. She couldn't give up on Jake, because that would be like giving up on herself.

But how to reach Jake was another matter. Without appearing to, Brenda studied her charge. The group session involved five kids including Jake. They'd been doing grounding exercises for a half hour. And so far, the only one of the five not to participate was Jake.

As she tried to figure out why he would not join in, a startling idea occurred to Brenda. Jake was an outlaw, or so he thought. The kids he hung out with were outlaws, too. Why not expose him to the other side of life? A better side where the system worked, where people were happy. If she showed him how others lived, and how they faced up to and dealt with real life situations, maybe his attitude would change. Perhaps she could help him see that there were other options available, besides anger and avoidance.

Excitement bubbled up, and Brenda felt as if she had another lease on life. When the session ended, and everyone started out, she pulled Jake aside.

"Another lecture?" he asked, staring at her through half lowered eyelids.

Brenda ignored his intense stare, as well as the

way her stomach tightened up. Instead, she concentrated on what she had to do. "No lecture," she told him. "I was just wondering if you'd like to get out of here for a little while."

Jake smiled. Brenda thought he looked even more handsome when he wasn't frowning. "With you?"

Brenda blinked. "Is that so terrible?"

"No, it's nice," Jake said, surprising her with the softness of his words. "Where do you want to go?"

"How about my house," she suggested spontaneously. "We can watch a movie on the VCR." Jake stared at her with a strange expression until Brenda became uncomfortable. "If you'd rather not. . . ."

"No, that sounds great. Besides, I'd like to see the inside of one of those Rose Hill houses."

Brenda gasped. "How did you know I live in Rose Hill?"

"I asked around," Jake said.

"Oh — " Shrugging, Brenda pushed aside the uneasy feeling his confession had brought out in her. "Well, then, let's go. I've got my mother's car."

They made the drive from Georgetown to Rose Hill in under thirty minutes. At three o'clock, Brenda opened the front door and led Jake inside. She didn't give him a full tour of the house, but she did walk him through the elegant dining room, and then into the large eat-in kitchen.

"Drink?" Brenda asked hesitantly.

"Sure," Jake replied. Dressed in worn jeans and a red T-shirt, Jake leaned against the kitchen

102

counter, hands in his pockets, studying the flowered wallpaper. His dark eyes scanned the room quickly, taking everything in. "Nice place," he commented.

"It's home," Brenda replied nonchalantly. But inside, her stomach churned. Six months ago she could never have said 'it's home.' Maybe in another six months, Jake will say the same thing about his parents' home, she thought hopefully.

Brenda poured two glasses of lemonade, and carried them into the den with Jake tagging behind. She put the glasses on the teak coffee table, and slipped two coasters beneath them. When she lifted her head, she saw Jake looking at the plaques on the far wall.

While he read the plaques, most of which had been awarded to her stepfather, Brenda looked over the movie collection. She selected Sean Penn's *Bad Boys*, because she wanted to see Jake's reaction to this particular movie. She hoped watching it together would lead them into a good discussion.

"Are you sure your parents aren't here?" Jake asked for the third time.

"I'm sure. What difference would it make if they were?"

Jake shrugged. He certainly was playing it cool, Brenda noticed. But she could sense his uncertainty nevertheless. Jake put on a big show, but here, where he was out of his own element, he was unsure, uncertain. His overconfident air was no longer as strong. For the first time since Brenda had met Jake, he appeared vulnerable.

He needs someone to help him, Brenda said to

herself. He's all alone and he won't admit that he doesn't like it.

"It must be great, living in a fancy house like this," Jake said when he finished reading the plaques and moved on to the bookcase on the far wall.

"It has its good points," Brenda agreed.

Jake turned slowly, his dark eyes locked on her. "Then why did you run away?"

Brenda didn't let Jake trap her. She wasn't going to do all the talking today — it was Jake's turn to tell her how he was feeling. "Why did you?" she asked, turning the tables.

"You said something about a movie," he reminded her, turning their confrontation into a draw.

Brenda sighed. "I did," she agreed. Going to the VCR, she slipped a cassette into its slot and turned the television on. When she returned to the couch with the remote control, Jake was sitting there, sipping his lemonade.

Brenda sat on the opposite end of the couch and pointed the remote control at the VCR. Before she could press the play button, she heard Chris's voice just outside the den.

Turning, she watched her stepsister and Phoebe saunter into the den, too deeply involved in their lively conversation to notice Brenda and Jake. But when Chris looked away from Phoebe, and saw Jake sitting on the couch, she froze. The short pleated skirt of her white tennis outfit fluttered in response to her sudden stop. Phoebe, following Chris's gaze, halted next to her friend.

"Hi," Brenda greeted them, covering her nervousness with a smile. "This is Jake Hoover, from Garfield House."

"Hi," Chris said in a subdued voice, "I'm Chris, this is Phoebe," she added pointing to Phoebe, who was dressed in a burgundy and white tennis outfit.

"Hi," Jake muttered without standing up.

Brenda did not miss the questioning glance that passed between Phoebe and Chris, and spoke to fill the sudden silence. "We were just getting ready to watch a movie," she explained, holding up the remote control in another nervous gesture. Darn it, why were they making her feel so jittery? Brenda wondered. This was her house, too, and she had the right to invite over anyone she wanted.

"Umm, we don't have time for a movie," Chris replied in a guarded voice, "but we'll join you for a few minutes." Sitting down awkwardly on the corduroy chair on Jake's right, Chris motioned Phoebe to come join them. Following her friend's lead, Phoebe parked herself on the matching chair to Brenda's left, tucking her legs beneath her before resting her hands on her lap.

Brenda glanced at Jake, and sensed that he was feeling very uncomfortable. Well, so was she. Trying to ease the tension, Brenda smiled at Chris. "Taking the day off from work?"

"They changed my schedule for the rest of the month to half days. Congressmen Barnes doesn't like to work his volunteers too hard." As she spoke, Chris's eyes continually moved from Brenda to Jake.

Brenda felt as if she and Jake were specimens under a microscope and Chris and Phoebe were on the other end. "Lucky you," Brenda said, trying her best not to show how upset she was getting. "Where's Ted?"

"He's at baseball practice."

Phoebe shifted in her chair. "How long have you been at Garfield House, Jake?"

The tone of her voice was challenging. Jake's eyes narrowed slightly, and he stared at Phoebe for a full ten seconds before answering, "Awhile."

"Oh," Phoebe stiffened for an instant before looking at Brenda. "How's Brad doing?" she asked bluntly.

Brenda felt a surge of irritation. How dare Phoebe question her like that! They weren't doing anything wrong. Yet, she couldn't get mad at Phoebe either, because she understood that her friend simply cared about what happened to both her and Brad.

"I haven't seen him since the party," Brenda admitted. "They switched his shift to the twelve to eight. By the time he gets home, he's really tired. But he's happy. You know Brad."

Before Phoebe could say anything else, Chris stood. "It was nice meeting you, Jake," she said with a smile. "Bren, did you leave my car keys in the kitchen? I promised Ted I'd pick him up at the ball field at Rosemont Park."

"On the key board," Brenda told her. "See you guys later."

When Chris and Phoebe were gone, Brenda reached for the remote control again. "Your sister seems nice. You get along well?" Jake asked, nonchalantly.

Brenda put down the remote. Maybe if she

told Jake a little about her family life, it might help him to open up to her.

"We do now. But at first, we didn't get along at all. I really resented her, because she was always Miss Perfect. I felt that she was always showing me up. But things changed."

"How?" Jake asked, his tone almost urgent.

As she looked at Jake, everything around them seemed to fade. The TV was forgotten, and her previous invitation, too, as Brenda found herself being drawn into his dark mysterious eyes. Her face felt hot as she stared at his lips, moist and slightly parted. He seemed almost to be inviting her to. . . . Brenda shook her head to break the spell and tried to concentrate on what she wanted to say.

"It wasn't until I realized that I was the one who was keeping everybody at a distance that things changed." Brenda continued. "I thought that no one wanted to bother with me, so I made myself believe that it was their fault and not mine."

"It usually is *their* fault," Jake commented knowingly.

"That's not true, Jake," Brenda stated. "You have to give other people a chance."

Jake shook his head. "You get hurt that way. Who's Brad?"

Jake's question caught her off guard. For a moment Brenda wondered if asking Jake over this afternoon had been a good idea. But she knew it was too late to change her mind now. "Brad Davidson. He's my boyfriend," she told him. "We've been going together for a while."

"What kind of job does he have?"

"It's a summer job at Montgomery Medical. He's an orderly on the preview to medical careers program. He's entering Princeton this year."

"Sounds like a real go-getter," Jake observed with a trace of sarcasm.

"He is," Brenda said, straightforwardly. "Brad's got things worked out for himself. I just wish — "

"Wish what?" Jake prodded and slowly moved closer to Brenda.

Brenda saw the movement and tensed. "Nothing."

"Hey, you're the one who's always pushing me to say what's on my mind. How can I, if you don't?"

Brenda was trapped by her own logic. She knew Jake was testing her, and that this could become an important point later on. She might even gain some leverage by being honest.

"Brad and I made a lot of plans, but his job keeps messing things up. He's working more hours than he was supposed to, which means he's constantly breaking our dates."

There was a pause, then Jake said, "I can't believe someone lucky enough to have a girl like you would be that stupid." His voice was suddenly gentle.

"He's not stupid," Brenda argued. "And it's not his fault."

"Sure it's his fault," Jake said as he slowly lifted his hand toward Brenda's face. When his fingers touched her cheek, as lightly as a butterfly's wings, she shivered. "You don't leave some-

108

one as pretty and as smart as you are sitting around doing nothing. I know I wouldn't."

"It's not like that," Brenda protested, trying to defend Brad, but feeling touched by his words just the same. "Besides, this is an important summer for Brad," she finished lamely.

"It's an important summer for me, too," Jake whispered.

Something in his voice made Brenda feel afraid. "Is being at Garfield House what makes the summer important for you?" Brenda asked at last. But again, Jake wouldn't answer.

"You shouldn't let anyone take you for granted," he said evasively.

"Brad doesn't take me for granted," Brenda argued.

"Oh, yeah? I'll tell you one thing: if you were my girl, I wouldn't break any dates," Jake murmured as he slid next to her. His hand rose to lightly cup her face, and sparks ignited along her skin.

Brenda felt dizzy. And she was beginning to feel out of control. Jake's hand on her cheek was maddening and wonderful at the same time. This is wrong, she told herself. She quickly stood up. "But I'm not your girl friend."

No sooner had she made it to her feet, than she heard footsteps in the hallway outside the den. She turned just as her stepfather entered the den.

"Hi. You're home early." Brenda greeted him breathlessly.

Jonathan Austin nodded. "The office air conditioning went out this morning. I lasted as long as I could."

"There's someone I'd like you to meet," Brenda informed him. "Jonathan Austin, this is Jake Hoover. Jake, this is my stepfather."

"Pleased to meet you, Jake," Jonathan said, going over to Jake and offering him his hand. "Brenda's mentioned you before."

When Jake stood to shake Jonathan's hand, Brenda noticed the vast difference between the two men. It was more than their clothing or their age, it was a contrast between someone who was self-confident and assured and someone who was out of his element.

While Jonathan looked Jake squarely in the eyes, Jake's eyes never quite met her stepfather's. Instead of speaking up clearly, Jake mumbled a greeting beneath his breath, and slouching, quickly put both hands back in the pockets of his jeans. Brenda was upset by his rudeness and spoke quickly in an effort to cover it up.

"I thought it would be a good idea if Jake got out of Garfield for a little while today," Brenda told her stepfather.

"It gets rough there sometimes, heh?" Jonathan asked Jake, his tone still friendly and warm.

Jake gave another mumbled reply and looked at Brenda. "I've got to get going to catch my bus," he said. "I don't want to miss curfew."

Before Brenda could point out that curfew wasn't until ten o'clock, Jake sped out of the den. She stared helplessly at her stepfather until they both heard the front door close.

"Very outgoing young man," Jonathan commented dryly.

Brenda sighed. "He's got a lot of problems. I guess parental authority is a big one. And —" she stopped herself quickly before she got into trouble.

"And what?" Jonathan asked, his stern features set in a scowl.

"I — uh — oh, boy," Brenda breathed, the blood rushing to her face. "And, you're a strong authority figure." She closed her eyes the minute she spoke the words. She didn't want to watch her stepfather's face when he exploded. When all Brenda heard was a throaty chuckle, she opened her eyes to see if her ears were deceiving her. They weren't. Her stepfather was smiling.

"I'm sure you'll be able to help him, Brenda," Jonathan said when he stopped laughing.

Brenda gazed into her stepfather's clear eyes, and felt relief and happiness wash over her. "I hope I can."

"I also thought we agreed that you wouldn't put your abilities down anymore," Jonathan stated.

"I know. But Jake's not easy to get through to."

"Anything worth doing, takes time," her stepfather informed her as he put his arm around Brenda's shoulders and gave her a gentle hug.

Glad that things had worked out so well between them, Brenda smiled. But she couldn't help adding, "Time is what I have plenty of this summer."

"Brad's working again tonight?"

Brenda shrugged. "Isn't he always?"

Jonathan shook his head. "Now you're sounding like your mother when I'm stuck at the office."

"That's the problem!" Brenda burst out.

A look of confusion flashed across her stepfather's face. "Excuse me?"

"I'm seventeen, and I'm going to be a high school senior. Why do I have to sound like my mother? And why does Brad have to act like — like — like an old man!" she cried. Unexpectedly, Brenda turned and fled from the den, leaving her stepfather behind, standing there bewildered.

Chapter 12

"Thanks, Brenda," Theresa said at the end of their private session.

"Any time. I've already told you that."

Theresa looked around Tony's office as she started to leave. "Uh. . . . You've been working with Jake Hoover, right?" she asked hesitantly.

"That's right. Everyone knows that," Brenda said, wondering what was going on in Theresa's mind.

"Yeah. Well, uh —"

"Are you having a problem with Jake?" Brenda asked, concerned for both Theresa and Jake.

Theresa shook her head quickly. "No, but he's . . . he's been hitting on a couple of the other girls. I thought that Eleanor Cortez and he had something going, but last night he was hanging out with Maryanne. Eleanor got really bent out of shape — you know how angry she can get."

Stunned by Theresa's words, Brenda fought to

keep her face expressionless. "I see. Well, make sure you keep out of Jake's way, okay?"

"No problem there. I've got too many other things to work out. I don't need boy trouble," Theresa sniffed. "See you," she added as she walked to the door. But once again, she paused and looked back at Brenda. "Will you be around later?"

Brenda shook her head. "I've got the afternoon off. A friend of mine is playing in an important baseball game. His team is tied for second place in the league. I'm going out to root for him."

"Sounds like fun," Theresa said with a wistful smile before leaving the office.

Brenda closed her eyes tightly. Theresa's gossip about Jake had unleashed strong feelings inside her. Brenda tried to tell herself that she was upset because anyone who came to Garfield House was there to work out their personal problems, not to find dates. It was hard to admit that she was hurt by what she had heard about Jake.

Finally, Brenda made herself stop thinking about Jake Hoover. Glancing at her watch, she saw it was noon; she had to leave soon. "Come on, Tony," she called to the door, wondering what was keeping him. Earlier, as they had passed in the hallway, Tony had told her he wanted to have a meeting with her before she left for the day.

When Tony did come into the office a few minutes later, she saw that he was smiling happily. "Hi, how's my favorite girl?"

"Ready to go to the ball game," Brenda said bluntly.

"I didn't forget," Tony said as he sat down in

114

the chair Theresa had just vacated. "This is a switch," he commented.

Brenda frowned. "What's a switch?"

"You sitting behind my desk, and me sitting in this chair."

Brenda started to get up, but Tony waved her back. "It's okay, you've earned the right to sit there. . . . Sometimes."

"Thanks," Brenda replied, wondering what Tony meant by his remark. "Tony?"

"I know, you want to get going. Just give me a few minutes, okay?"

When Brenda nodded, Tony's eyes took on a faraway look that Brenda recognized as his way of working through a problem. "Don't take this the wrong way," he began.

Immediately, every muscle in Brenda's body stiffened. "Take what the wrong way?"

"Brenda, I know how hard you're working with Jake, and I know that getting through to him means a lot to you. But I think you're overdoing it."

"He needs more help," Brenda stated adamantly.

"How many sessions have you had with him?" Tony asked in a tight voice.

Brenda looked out the window for a moment. "He's not easy to pin down," she began lamely.

"Brenda," Tony said, raising one eyebrow, "I'm not blind. Jake's been avoiding you, and you spend most of your time following him and watching him."

"But I am making some headway," Brenda said defensively.

"Maybe. But, Brenda, does he want more help? Look, you took on certain responsibilities when you asked to work here over the summer. Until you started with Jake, you were doing fine. The extra time you're spending with Jake takes you away from the others who genuinely need you — you're sacrificing all the good work you've accomplished with the others because of Jake."

"That's not true," Brenda retorted. "I just spent a half hour with Theresa."

Tony nodded. "Did you know that Carla had another crisis yesterday?"

"She what?" Brenda asked, stunned.

"She had a fight with her mother, and ended up here about four o'clock, looking for you."

"I — "

"It happens, Brenda. You can't be here for everyone all the time. You have to balance the good with the bad. You asked to work with Jake. You weren't assigned to him. Please don't forget about the kids who *really* depend on you."

"I'm sorry, Tony," Brenda whispered. "It's just that Jake has so much potential."

"I don't doubt Jake has all the potential you credit him with. But, Brenda, you're losing sight of one thing . . ." Tony paused to stare directly into Brenda's eyes. "You have to remember that *you* can't change him. Jake has to want to work things out for himself."

Brenda closed her eyes for a moment. "I can't just give up on him."

"I'm not asking you to. But I want you to remember the others also. Can you do that?"

Brenda opened her eyes and smiled. "Yes, I can," she declared.

"Good. Now get out of here and go watch Ted hit a home run if he's not still trying to kick the baseball through the goalposts," Tony joked.

The sun was bright and hot over Rose Hill Park. The air was dry, and the sounds of the people in the bleachers was loud. The Orioles were playing Ted's team, the Ramblers. It was the fourth inning, and the score was tied five to five.

Brenda, sitting with Chris, Phoebe, Monica, and Woody, was enjoying the game, and had temporarily pushed aside her problems at Garfield House.

"I can't believe the Ramblers are playing so well," Brenda said to Chris. "No one thought they would win more than a few games."

"I know," Chris agreed enthusiastically, looking toward the dugout where Ted was standing. Beneath the Ramblers' baseball cap Chris wore, her eyes were proud. "Can you believe how good Ted's gotten? I mean," Chris added as the last of the Ramblers struck out and the team started out onto the field again, "Ted was ready to give it all up."

"But he didn't," Brenda reminded her stepsister.

"Because of you," Chris stated gratefully. "If you hadn't been there for Ted to talk with, he would have given up baseball, and he would have given up on me, too."

"No, he wouldn't," Brenda protested quickly.

Chris reached over and took Brenda's hand. When she looked at Brenda, her eyes were moist. "I really am lucky to have a sister like you."

Brenda was embarrassed for a moment, but she also felt warmly toward her sister. "Me, too," she whispered.

"Brenda," Phoebe called. Letting go of Chris's hand, Brenda looked over to Phoebe. "What happened with that guy you had over the house the other day?"

Brenda tensed at Phoebe's words. "Happened?"

"Yes. I mean what's his story? Is he working his problems out? He sure didn't look too comfortable when we got there."

"Jake's trying to deal with a lot of stuff right now."

"Hmm. I wonder, though, if maybe one of his problems is you," Phoebe suggested.

Caught off guard, Brenda drew up her defenses. "Me? I'm trying to help him."

"Oh, I know you are, Brenda. But from the way he was looking at you, I think his idea of help isn't exactly the same as yours."

"What is that supposed to mean?" Brenda asked, half standing to glare at Phoebe. Then she felt Chris's cool hand on her arm.

"Take it easy," Chris cautioned.

"No I won't," she told Chris. "Come on Phoebe. What are you trying to say?"

"Nothing, Brenda." Phoebe said, relenting. "I just guess I was surprised to see Jake with you instead of Brad. I'm sorry."

The anger drained from Brenda as fast as it

had come. "It's okay, Phoebe, I'm sorry, too. It's just that everyone is down on Jake and implying all kinds of things, and all I'm trying to do is to make him see things differently. He's not as bad as he seems. It's all an act."

"Is it?" Phoebe couldn't resist asking. All at once, a strange expression washed across her face. "Uh, oh," Phoebe whispered.

The loud rumbling of a motorcycle echoed in the air of the bleachers. Turning quickly, Brenda saw Jake Hoover, astride a black bike, come sliding to a fast stop just below her, where the parking lot ended and the bleachers began.

What's he doing here? she asked herself, her stomach knotting with worry. When Jake got off the motorcycle, after gunning it noisily several times, he took off his helmet and looked up at them.

Reluctantly, Brenda waved to him. He waved back and started around to the side of the bleachers.

"What's he doing here?" Chris whispered.

"I don't know," Brenda replied. When Chris gave her a questioning look, Brenda shook her head. "I really don't. I didn't even tell him about the game."

A moment later, Jake was moving up the bleachers toward her. Brenda couldn't help noticing the hard line of his mouth, the unyielding set of his head, and the dangerous glint in his eyes. His renegade outfit — black jeans, motorcycle boots, and black cut-off T-shirt — only served to emphasize his bold good looks.

Glancing to her right, she saw Phoebe's and Woody's heads together. Woody's curious eyes followed Jake's every step.

"So this is how you spend your days in Rose Hill," Jake commented, coming up beside her.

"One of the ways," Brenda replied. "You remember my sister, Chris, and my friend, Phoebe?"

"Sure," Jake said without even a hello to the two girls.

"That's Woody next to Phoebe. Monica is the blonde on the other side."

"That's nice."

Brenda stiffened at his tone, but forced herself to be patient. "Why don't you sit down and join us? I didn't know you liked baseball."

Jake laughed and looked out at the field just as a batter hit a long fly ball. Ted, who was playing center field today, went after it. So did the right fielder. When they both met with a crash, the ball fell behind them. Chris groaned loudly.

"Is that baseball?" Jake asked, squinting at the disaster on the field. His words were spoken loudly, and several kids turned to look at them. Embarrassed by Jake's comment, Brenda's cheeks burned.

"There's no call for that," she reprimanded him.

One corner of Jake's mouth curled upward. "You're right. One of those bozos should have caught the ball."

"Jake — " she began, but he cut her off.

"Look, I came here because I wanted to talk with you, not watch baseball. Can we talk?" he asked, abruptly.

120

It wasn't the stare, or even the dark mystery behind his eyes, it was the knowledge that Jake had sought her out that made Brenda agree. He wanted to talk to her, and she couldn't turn down any opportunity to be near him.

"All right." Standing, she looked down at Chris. "I'll be back later."

Chris reached up and grabbed Brenda's wrist. "Will you be okay?" she whispered.

"Sure," Brenda told her with more confidence than she felt. Avoiding the eyes of her friends, she made her way down the bleachers.

Jake led her to the spot where he'd parked his black Honda Shadow. "What do you think?" he asked, leaning casually on the bike.

"About what?"

"The bike," Jake said, waving his hand over the seat.

"Nice. Looks dangerous though."

"Nah, not if you know what you're doing. And I know what I'm doing with this baby." His fingers caressed the handlebars while he spoke.

Brenda shivered as she watched the loving way he touched the bike. She had a fleeting curiosity about the way those fingers would feel on her skin.

Taking a deep breath, Brenda said, "You wanted to talk to me?"

"Yeah. I thought we would be having a session this afternoon."

"I never told you that."

"You've asked me to have a session every day," he reminded her. And you've refused to cooperate every time, Brenda was tempted to say. But she remained silent. Looking into Jake's dark eyes, she wondered if she had been wrong to come to the game, instead of staying at Garfield House. Wasn't he really asking her for help? "Okay, we're together now, let's talk."

Jake stared silently at her, until Brenda started to feel nervous. "What did you want to talk about?" she asked again.

"Nothing."

"You didn't come here for nothing. Please talk to me, Jake. I want to help you."

Jake continued to stare at Brenda for a moment longer. "That's nice, what you said. That you want to help me."

"I do. What's going on, Jake?"

In the second it took for Brenda to ask the question, Jake's eyes became distant. "I don't know. . . . It's just that I'm starting to feel uncomfortable at Garfield House."

"Why?"

Jake shrugged. "Who knows. Tony, I guess. That guy is always on my case. He never lets up!"

"He's not supposed to, Jake. He doesn't let up because he cares."

"Sure — about himself. About the way he wants everyone to look up to him. He wants everyone to become the same so that every kid he helps is his personal success story. C'mon, Brenda, the guy's head is swelled all out of proportion."

"That's not fair," Brenda cried angrily. "Tony is one of the good guys. He just believes in discipline. If you'd ease up a little, you'd see that for yourself."

"The only good guy I've met at Garfield House is you," he shot back at her.

Brenda's next words stuck to her tongue. She stared at him for several seconds, trying to think of what to say. "Jake, we're all good guys. Even you," she whispered at last.

"Sure," he said, turning away from her.

"Don't shut me out, Jake," Brenda pleaded, sensing that she had lost him again.

Jake fixed his eyes on her, a strange expression on his face. "Not me. I'd never shut *you* out." With that, he mounted his bike, turned the ignition on, and started the engine. "See you," he called out.

With a scream of his rear tire, Jake took off. Brenda watched him drive away, all too aware that somehow she had failed him. And if *she* had failed him, where in the world did Jake have left to go?

Chapter
13

It was a clear and beautiful summer night in Fairfax, Virginia, home of the Wolftrap concert amphitheater. Brenda, wearing navy blue leotards, pale blue Reeboks, and a button-down extra-large white shirt belted tightly around her waist, sat between Brad and Peter. Monica, wearing white slacks and a lavender top, sat on Peter's right.

They were camped on the gently sloping hill that rose upward from the covered area of the concert stage. The grass beneath Brenda was warm and soft. The only light coming from the amphitheater was from the spotlights over the white lacquered grand piano on the stage.

A low rustling of voices permeated the air, as the audience awaited the pianist who was performing tonight. Wolftrap was almost full, and the covered seating section nearest the stage was packed. The open seating areas, outside of the sheltered seats, were just as full.

Wolftrap's clamshell-like appearance was an awesome, magnificent sight that always left Brenda a little breathless. Every time she came here to hear a concert, she was amazed by the quality of the sound. She could invariably hear every note, just as well as if she were sitting in a closed auditorium where the music was amplified by powerful electronics.

"This was a great idea," Brad said, shifting around so he could lay down and rest his head on Brenda's lap. "I just wish I wasn't as tired as I am."

"So do I," Brenda murmured, thinking that after four days of looking forward to tonight, all Brad could do was complain about how tired he was.

And, on the trip to Wolftrap from Rose Hill, Monica had monopolized the conversation with stories about how great it was to work at K-100, and how professionally everything was done. Peter, she recalled, had said very little. He'd spent most of the ride staring out his window. Brenda sympathized with him completely, knowing what it was like to have your date talk only about work.

Once they had parked the car, and walked to a section of the hill that gave them a clear view of the stage, they'd found a little encampment and set the cooler down in front of them.

The stage was not brightly lit. A lone figure, dressed in a white evening jacket, walked toward the piano. The applause grew loud. But the minute the pianist sat on his bench, all sound ceased. An instant later, he struck the first notes. Soon, the air was filled with the beautiful notes of the first sonata.

Brenda forgot everything: Brad's tiredness, Jake's rebelliousness, and even Ted and the Ramblers' baseball loss that afternoon. As the music floated over her, she closed her eyes and let herself be lulled by the magical sound of the piano.

When the sonata ended, Brenda did not open her eyes. Instead, she breathed deeply while waiting for the next piece to begin. Her hand rested on Brad's shoulder, his head stayed comfortably still in her lap.

Just as the next piece started, and began to build into the strong and powerful chords that Beethoven was known for, Peter nudged Brenda.

Jarred out of her reverie, Brenda looked at Peter, who pointed to Brad. When she looked down at her lap, she saw Brad's eyes were closed and his chest was rising and falling evenly.

Brad was sound asleep! Then Peter pointed to Monica, who was jotting down notes on a piece of paper, oblivious to everything around her.

"Do you believe her?" Peter asked in a low voice. "If she isn't talking about her show, she's working on it."

"She reminds me of someone else." Brenda nodded at Brad. "If he's not working, he's sleeping."

Peter leaned closed to Brenda, and said conspiratorially, "We ought to leave them here and

126

go find other seats. That would teach them a lesson."

Brenda giggled. "I'd love to, but if I move, Brad will wake up."

"You know, Brenda, I don't know if I can handle much more of this. I feel like I created a monster when I took Monica on as my assistant."

"She's just caught up in the excitement of her job," Brenda said, wanting to make Peter feel better.

"Is that what you tell yourself when you're out with Brad?" Peter asked, surprising her with the intensity of his words.

For a moment, Brenda considered lying. Turning to Peter, she confessed, "Yes, that's what I try to tell myself."

"It doesn't work too well, does it?"

Brenda exhaled sharply. "No, it doesn't," she admitted. "But have you tried to talk to her about it? Let her know how you feel?"

Peter shrugged his shoulders. "I don't want to hurt her," he said. Then he shook his head sharply. "No, that's not it. I guess I'm mad that she's not sensitive enough to realize what she's doing, and I also want her to need me more than her show."

Brenda couldn't find any words of comfort for him. Peter's open admission struck her deeply, for he had voiced the exact thing that was bothering her about Brad. Suddenly, her anger got the best of her. Moving quickly, she pushed Brad's head off her lap.

"Hey!" Brad shouted, waking up when his head hit the earth.

"Quiet!" hissed a man sitting nearby.

"The concert's on. Why don't you try to listen?" Brenda told Brad as she made herself watch the pianist. But the evening had been ruined for Brenda. She felt only anger now.

When the concert was over, and the four headed to the parking lot, Brad took Brenda's hand in his. "Did you enjoy it?"

"It could have been better," Brenda said, not thinking about the concert but about Brad. What she wanted to say was: You could have made it better.

"Gee," Monica broke in. "I thought it was very good. I was going to talk a little about it on Sunday's show. After all, the station did give me the tickets."

"The pianist was excellent," Brenda said. "I just would have preferred my date to be awake."

"Give me a break, Brenda," Brad pleaded. "I've — "

" — been working hard at the hospital," Brenda finished for him. "Well, you know what, Brad?" she shouted, stopping in the middle of the crowd. "I've been working hard, too. But I don't fall asleep when we're together!"

"Bren, you don't understand," Brad started to say, but once again, Brenda cut him off.

"Maybe I do."

"What are you getting at?" Brad asked, his lips thinning into a tight line.

Before Brenda's temper got completely out of control, she took a deep calming breath. I'm not getting at anything," she said. "I'm just . . . frustrated."

128

"About what?" Brad asked. Reaching out, he took Brenda's hand in his and looked deeply into her eyes.

"About Garfield House," she said, only half truthfully.

"Want to talk about it?" Brad asked.

"I'd like that. I need to talk to someone."

Brad looked around and saw that Peter and Monica were already at the car. "Come on, we'll talk on the way back to Rose Hill."

At the car, Peter and Monica got into the backseat. Brenda climbed into the passenger seat beside Brad, and once he manuevered the silver Honda onto the highway, she turned eagerly to him. "Ready to listen?"

"I'm always ready to listen," Brad stated with a straight face. Brenda ignored Peter's cough. "There's this guy I'm working with. I told you about him before."

"I don't remember you talking about any guy. I thought you worked with the girls."

"I try and help any of the kids at Garfield House," Brenda corrected him, annoyed that he had already forgotten the talk they'd had last week.

"What kind of a guy is he?" Brad asked quickly.

"The usual: He's lonely and he'd kind of an outlaw."

Brad glanced at her for a moment, and Brenda knew he had detected the slight change of tone when she had spoken. "Where's he from?"

"Cartwell."

Brad shook his head. "That's not a good area.

129

A lot of rough kids come from there."

"Jake's not rough," Brenda said quickly. "He's just alone."

"I don't know. Since I've been at the hospital, I've seen at least a dozen of those tough guys from Cartwell in the emergency room — knife fights, car accidents. You know, there was this bad case yesterday — " Brad began.

"Stop it!" Brenda ordered, infuriated that Brad had started talking about the hospital again.

Brad stopped talking.

Brad nodded. "Sorry, I just get carried away. Go ahead, tell me about Jack."

"Jake," Peter corrected Brad from the back-seat.

Monica looked up at that moment, confused. "Who's Jake?" she asked.

"Nobody," Brad told her.

"Isn't he the guy who came by the game today, Brenda? The one on the black motorcycle?" Monica asked.

Brenda closed her eyes for a second when Brad glanced at her. "Yes," she said.

"Oh," Monica added before leaning her head back onto Peter's shoulder.

"And Brad," Brenda said in a firm voice, "he's not a *nobody*, he's *somebody*. That's the problem. No one thinks he matters." Brenda paused to gain control over her emotions. She knew she was treading on dangerous ground, and could not let her feelings show too strongly.

"That's why he's what we call an outlaw — someone who works hard not to fit in anywhere," she explained.

"Why did he come to Rose Hill?" Brad asked, distractedly, as he adjusted the rearview mirror.

"Because he needed to talk to me," Brenda said in a tight voice. Which is more than you need me for, she added silently when she saw that Brad's concentration was once again fixed on the road ahead. He doesn't even care enough to be jealous, she realized sadly.

After dropping Monica and Peter off, and after promising Monica that she would get together with her the following afternoon to discuss the topics for her interview, they drove to Brenda's house.

At the front door, Brad took Brenda in his arms. "Bren, I'm sorry about falling asleep at the concert. I am tired, but I *wanted* to be with you."

"That's what you always say," Brenda charged, unable to keep her frustrations contained.

"And I mean it. It's just. . . ." Brad shrugged. "When I get involved with something, I have to give all of my self. You do the same thing with Garfield House. Forgive me?" he whispered as he bent and kissed her deeply.

His arms held her so close to his chest that she could feel his heart beating. But even though his lips pressed heatedly upon hers, Brenda could not forget her anger and frustration. When the kiss ended, Brenda opened her eyes and stared boldly up at Brad. "Please don't take me for granted, Brad."

"I never do," he reassured her.

"Oh, I almost forgot," Brenda said. "Chris asked if we wanted to go with her and Ted to the movies Saturday night."

131

"Sure," Brad replied with a smile. "But you know what I can't wait for?"

"What?"

"A chance to show you how much I appreciate you." Brad kissed Brenda again, even more softly, and Brenda became lost in the moment.

Chapter
14

At one o'clock in the afternoon, Brad was pushing an empty wheelchair down the hall of Montgomery Medical Center. He was bringing it back to the emergency room.

Brad was tired from the first five hours of his shift. As soon as he finished delivering the chair, he was going to take his lunch hour.

"Excuse me, Doctor," said an elderly man, a few feet away.

Before Brad could tell the man he was only an orderly, the man went on. "I'm looking for the x-ray room and I seem to have gotten lost."

"Make a left at the next corner," Brad informed him. "It will be the third door on the right."

"Thank you, Doctor," the man said.

"I'm not a — " But the man was already walking away from him. " — doctor, *yet*." Smiling at his thoughts of the future, Brad continued on to the emergency room.

Opening the door, he pushed the wheelchair into the emergency room, which he discovered was empty. He glanced at the vacant rows of chairs lining the walls, and thought he'd never seen the room so quiet. Usually, there were at least half a dozen people waiting to see a doctor.

As he deposited the chair next to two others, the loud wailing of an ambulance's siren broke the silence. The nurse behind the desk glanced up expectantly at the ambulance entry doors on the far side of the emergency room.

Following the nurse's gaze, Brad saw the emergency room doctor and another nurse rush to the entrance. A half minute later, the double doors burst open, and two paramedics wheeled in a gurney. Behind them came a Maryland State Trooper.

"Watch the desk," the nurse ordered Brad as she sped toward the policeman. For a moment, Brad was paralyzed. Everything was happening so fast, all he could do was stare. Quickly, the medical team surrounded the paramedics — one glance at the patient was enough to tell Brad that the accident victim was in bad shape. All at once he found his legs again and hurried over to stand behind the desk.

"What happened?" the doctor asked, checking the unconscious man's eyes as the gurney moved toward the first cubicle.

The policeman looked at the doctor. "He's one of those crazy bikers from Cartwell. He ran head on into a car. He must have been doing fifty." He shook his head wearily.

The gurney was almost opposite Brad, and he

couldn't help staring at the biker. When he saw the amount of blood on the young man's face, his stomach almost turned inside out. He wanted to look away, but he couldn't, and continued to watch.

At the same moment, the street entry door opened. A woman looking upset and frightened came into the emergency room carrying a small child. Just as she reached Brad, the desk nurse returned, and Brad breathed a sigh of relief.

"I'll handle this," she told Brad. "But we're shorthanded right now. You'd better go over there in case they need something."

"I'm just an orderly," Brad reminded her.

The nurse shook her head quickly. "It doesn't matter, at least you're not a patient. Please go over in case the doctor needs help."

Nervously, Brad made his way over the cubicle and stood hesitantly just inside its entrance. In the time since the gurney had entered the room, the nurse had stripped most of the biker's clothing away, and the doctor was working on his chest. Brad's stomach turned queasy again. He clenched his teeth tightly.

"If I see another one of these motorcycle accidents, I think I'm going to quit medicine," the doctor claimed, cleaning one of the deep wounds just above the patient's abdomen. She was an attractive but tired-looking woman in her mid-forties, Brad guessed. He wondered just how many accidents the doctor had seen. Were they all as bad as this one?

"Don't become a policeman," remarked the officer.

"He's going to need blood," the doctor stated.

Suddenly Brad remembered the conversation he'd had with Brenda on the way home from Wolftrap. The guy she counseled at Garfield House was from Cartwell, and he drove a motorcycle. He remembered the boy's name. It was Jake.

The policeman was looking through the biker's wallet. "His blood type is B positive. He's seventeen, and his name is Chuck Parkins." Brad breathed a sigh of relief that it wasn't Brenda's friend.

"Orderly. Call for three units of whole blood. Type B. Stat!" shouted the doctor. When Brad didn't respond, she shouted, "Orderly!" again.

Brad's eyes snapped open. He stared at the doctor's gloved hand and the blood-drenched swab in her fingers. "Now!" commanded the doctor.

"Th-three units, type B?" Brad stammered.

The nurse looked up then and added, "Dial 6755."

Brad shook himself forcefully, turned, and tried to push the image of the injured biker from his eyes as he dialed the number and requested the blood, stat.

"We're losing him," one of the paramedics cried.

Brad whirled, his eyes were wide and his mouth was filled with a bitter taste.

"Get the crash cart!" the doctor ordered as she released what was in her hands and started giving the patient CPR. The nurse raced out into the emergency room.

Brad turned and held back the green curtain that blocked off the cubicle from the rest of the emergency room so that the crash cart would not get caught on the material. Behind him, he heard the doctor pressing on the patient's chest.

The nurse returned on a run, pushing the chrome cart that was filled with electronic leads and digital readouts.

Brad watched as the nurse set up the cart, and the paramedics put a board beneath the unmoving form of the biker. The nurse handed the doctor the two rounded electric shock paddles, and set the amperage the doctor called for.

"Clear!" the doctor shouted as she pressed the paddles to the biker's chest. Brad's breath caught when the thin frame of the injured man spasmed on the table.

For fifteen minutes, the doctor alternated between electric shock and CPR in her effort to save the boy's life. But when the green phosphorescent lines on the cardio-monitor stayed flat, the doctor finally shook her head sadly and shut the machine off.

Brad leaned against the wall as a wave of dizziness swept through him. "Stupid kids. When are they going to learn that a motorcycle is no match for a two-ton car," Brad heard her mutter.

Suddenly, Brad realized that the doctor was staring at him. "He could have been a friend of yours! He's your age. I hope you have more sense than this."

Brad knew the doctor was upset at having lost the boy, but her harsh words affected him deeply. Brad shook his head, unable to speak, yet unable to take his eyes from the dead boy. He had never seen someone die before. He realized that he was trembling violently, and as his stomach twisted, Brad knew he couldn't stay in the cubicle any longer.

Racing out of the cubicle and the emergency room, Brad fled to the safety of the employee's lounge, where he sat huddled in a corner away from the other people taking their breaks. Although he was on his lunch hour, even the thought of food made him feel sick.

Forty-five minutes later, when his break was over, Brad felt a little better. But he couldn't stop thinking about Brenda. For some reason, being upset made him want desperately to be with her. He wanted to see Brenda, to feel her in his arms right then. He knew she would understand why he was so upset, and give him the comfort and strength he needed.

"Tonight," he promised himself as he got to his feet wearily and left the lounge. The rest of his shift would be spent helping out in physical therapy. As he reached the elevator, the chrome doors opened. Stepping inside he found himself face to face with Mr. Greer.

"Have a good lunch, Davidson?" Mr. Greer asked pleasantly.

Brad shook his head. "I wasn't hungry."

"Make sure you eat dinner then, you're going to need some fortification to make it through tonight's seminar."

Brad stared at him as if he was crazy. "Seminar?"

"It's been on the bulletin board all week,

Davidson. Doctor Gordon is speaking on internal medicine. It's for all preview to medical career students."

Mr. Greer's words filtered into Brad's ears like a dark and ominous cloud. No, it can't be true — not tonight, Brad thought. He didn't want to go to a seminar, he wanted to see Brenda. He knew what he had to say; he wasn't going to let Brenda down again. "Mr. Greer," he said, "I can't make it tonight."

Mr. Greer stared at Brad for several seconds. "Yes you can," the supervisor replied in no uncertain terms. "That's the way the preview program works. Either you follow it completely, or you drop out of it. There's no in-between."

It was obvious from the stony expression on his supervisor's face that any argument was pointless. Sighing with frustration, Brad said, "I'll be there."

"I know you will," Mr. Greer stated, just as the elevator stopped on the second floor and Brad was able to escape.

"It's not fair," Brad muttered angrily under his breath. Reluctantly, he walked toward the pay phone across from the elevators. Brenda had told him she would be home all day today, and he decided he might as well get the bad news over with. "Again," he said aloud as he put a quarter into the telephone.

The kitchen phone rang. Brenda put down the cookbook she had been studying. She'd been going through her favorite recipes in anticipation of the dinner she was going to cook for Brad next

Saturday night. Hopping off the counter stool, she skipped across the floor to the wall phone. Picking it up, she offered a cheery, "Hello."

"Hi, Brenda."

The instant she heard his voice, she knew something was wrong. "Are you okay?" she asked immediately.

"Sure, I'm fine," he told her. "But I have some bad news."

Brenda's smile dissolved. Her hand tightened on the telephone. "What?"

"There's another seminar tonight. It's mandatory for preview students. I have to be there."

"Right!" Brenda shouted.

"Brenda, I tried to get out of it, I really did. It's not my fault this time."

Brenda closed her eyes and shook her head angrily. "It's never your fault," she said sadly. "Canceling our date with Chris and Ted on Saturday night wasn't your fault. You had to work a second shift. Monday night you had a lecture you forgot about. I suppose you want to cancel dinner next Saturday, too?"

"Come on, Brenda. You know I don't have any choice·about the seminars — they're required. I have to go to them. And I already promised I wouldn't cancel this Saturday night."

Opening her eyes, Brenda stared at the ceiling without saying a word. She heard some noise in the background on the other end of the line.

"Brenda, I've got to get back to work. I love you," Brad told her.

"See you," Brenda whispered when she hung up the phone. "Maybe."

Going back to the counter, she slammed the cookbook shut. "I hate you, Brad Davidson — that's the third broken date in a row!" she shouted. "And I'm not going to cry! You won't make me cry again."

Brenda put her head in her hands. She hadn't seen Brad in almost a week, not since they'd gone to Wolftrap. She had tried to be understanding, but it was getting harder and harder to watch her friends having fun while she stayed home alone. Chris had tried to help by inviting Brenda to come along with her and Ted each time they went out, but she had refused.

"I'm not staying home alone anymore," Brenda promised herself.

Suddenly, the kitchen walls started to close in on her. If she stayed inside one more minute Brenda knew she would start sobbing. In a flash, she thought of Rosemont Park.

After putting her mother's cookbook away, Brenda shut off the light in the kitchen and went to the front door. As she reached for the doorknob, the bell rang.

When she opened the door, Brenda gasped. Jake Hoover stood on her doorstep. His straight black hair gleamed in the afternoon sun, and he was smiling.

Brenda swallowed several times before she was able to smile. "Hi, this is a surprise," she said when she finally found her voice. "I was just going out."

"To where?" Jake asked, looked openly at Brenda's taupe shorts and white short sleeve safari shirt. "Nice outfit."

141

"Thanks. I was going to talk a walk over to Rosemont Park."

"Mind if I tag along?"

"I don't mind," she said as she closed the front door behind her. "Is something wrong?"

"Why?"

Brenda shrugged. "Because you came all the way over here to see me."

"I was in the neighborhood, so I thought I'd stop by."

"Oh. . . . That's nice," Brenda added after thinking how unusual it was for Jake to be anywhere in Rose Hill at all. But that thought was soon forgotten as they walked together toward the park.

In the park, they stayed away from the most crowded areas and went to the place Brenda liked best. It was at the southern end of the park, away from the large old mansion and the formal gardens. Brenda stopped at a secluded spot near the high stone fence. They were surrounded by elm trees, cherry trees, and silence.

"I love this place," she confided. "When I need to get away from everyone, I come here, and it makes me feel better."

"I like the way you look leaning on that tree," Jake said, his voice low and husky as he stepped closer to her. A lock of his dark hair fell onto his forehead.

Brenda shivered. She felt trapped by his gaze. "Jake, I. . . ." she began, but couldn't go on. What's happening to me? she asked herself when she realized that she didn't want to escape from him.

142

"You're the prettiest girl I've ever known," Jake told her as he moved closer. "The minute I saw you at Garfield House, I knew I wanted to be with you." Brenda could feel the heat from his body, he was so near. A strange lethargy came over her, and she leaned back against the tree, watching Jake.

Slowly Jake lifted his arms. For an instant, Brenda thought he was going to embrace her. But he didn't; rather, his hands slipped past her face, and came to rest on the tree.

"Jake," Brenda whispered huskily as she shook her head. His eyes were dark and lively.

It was hard to breathe and there was a buzzing in her ears. His breath on her cheek sent a chill through her body. "Brenda," Jake said, "I've never felt this way about any girl before."

Her mind spun. "No, Jake," she whispered, fighting the emotions that were mounting within her. "This is wrong."

"It's not wrong, Brenda. The way I feel about you can't be wrong. And you feel something for me, too."

Brenda remembered what Theresa had said about Jake the other day. "Is that what you told the girls at Garfield House?" she asked, her voice edged with irritation.

Jake raised his eyebrows. "They didn't mean anything to me, Brenda. I was bored. They were just company."

"Jake."

"I can't help myself, Brenda. You do things to me that make me crazy."

Brenda knew what he meant. She felt that way,

143

too. For a second, she thought about the last time she had felt like this. It had been a long, long time ago, when she and Brad had first started dating. Just thinking about Brad got her mad again. When Jake's hands left the tree and drifted down her sides, she realized that she had no desire — and no strength — to run away from him.

Two heartbeats later, escape was impossible. Jake's hands tightened around her, as he drew her close. An instant later, his lips covered hers.

Brenda's heart pounded. Her head was swimming, and she had to close her eyes to keep herself from falling down. Yet, the tingling that was racing along her skin told her that even if what was happening was wrong, it was wonderful at the same time.

When Jake pulled away a moment later, Brenda opened her eyes. Jake was staring at her, his eyes hooded. "I'm glad I came over to see you today," he said.

"So-so am I," she admitted reluctantly.

The corners of Jake's mouth curved upward. His hands rose until they cupped her face. Slowly, he pulled her to him and kissed her again.

The tingling inside Brenda increased. As her body melted against Jake's, and her arms wound around his back, she forgot about Brad. She forgot about everything but the feel of Jake's kisses. The sunlight and the cool open woods, and the warmth of his body mingled together in a glorious blur of sensation.

An instant later, Brenda and Jake slid down the trunk of the tree and sank onto the warm grass without once letting go of each other.

Chapter
15

Wednesday afternoon was Peter's day off. He spent the morning cataloging his record collection, putting them into the filing system in the Apple computer, which he'd gotten as a birthday present from his folks. When he'd taken his first computer course at school, Peter had found that he had a natural talent for programming, and now, next to music, his second biggest interest was computer programming.

Just as he finished entering his last album notation, the phone rang. Peter glanced at the clock hanging above his Springsteen poster. It was one-thirty.

"Hello," he said when he picked up the phone.

"Hi," Monica replied. "Are you working hard?"

"I just finished."

"Oh, good," Monica said. "Why don't you come over to my place?"

Peter looked at the screen of his computer for a second, trying to find an excuse to avoid Monica. "Well — " he began, but Monica cut him off.

"I have a neat surprise for you," she said in a teasing tone.

"Surprise, huh?" Peter replied, his interest perking even though he was upset with Monica. "What kind of a surprise?"

Peter heard Monica giggle. He liked the way her light laugh sounded. "It won't be a surprise if I tell you, will it?"

"Sure it will," Peter said, joining in on her game.

"Uh-uh, you'll just have to come over to my place to find out."

"Okay. I'm on my way." Peter replied, giving in.

"See you soon."

Now what? Peter asked himself as he shut off his computer and started out of his room. On the drive over, Peter was beset by conflicting emotions. His problem was simple: He loved her, and he didn't want to break up with her, but spending time with such an obsessed Monica was making him want to do just that. Was avoiding her the answer though?

When he got out of the car, he saw Monica was waiting outside for him. As he walked toward her, he couldn't help but notice how beautiful she was. Her blond hair shone in the sunlight, framing her pixielike face. Her hazel eyes were all aglow.

When he reached her, she almost jumped into his arms, with a quick kiss. "Well?" she asked.

"Well, what?"

Monica sighed. "Aren't you going to ask me what the surprise is?"

"What's the surprise?" Peter asked dutifully.

"Boy, I get more curiosity from my cat," she said, pouting.

"It's hard to be curious when I'm almost starving to death. I didn't eat lunch yet," he explained, hiding his true feelings of his doubts about coming over to Monica's.

Monica looked coyly at him. "Do you want some lunch first?"

With Monica's teasing glance, Peter let himself get into the rhythm of their game. Smiling slyly he said, "Sure, why don't we go over to the sub shop?"

"I'm not hungry," Monica said with another pout. She reached for a plain white envelope lying on the side of the table. She picked it up with her delicate fingers and offered it to him.

"What is it?" he asked, reaching for it.

"Your surprise," Monica said in exasperation. "Open it!"

Peter carefully lifted the unsealed flap. Inside he saw two rectangular objects.

"Take them out," Monica prodded.

Peter did, and when he read the first line, his eyes grew as wide as silver dollars. "Oh, wow," he whispered, staring at the rarest tickets in town. They were for the opening concert of Springsteen's new tour, which would start in August.

When he looked at Monica, all he could do was grin.

"Did I surprise you?" Monica asked, even

though her eyes told him she knew she had.

Peter was so tongue-tied he was glad he wasn't in the middle of a radio show. "How did you — I mean — "

Monica laughed lightly. "K-100 got a block of tickets. They gave me two."

As the words reached his ears, Peter's cheerful mood slipped. "Thanks, Monica," he said, forcing himself to keep smiling.

Before Monica could reply, her younger sister Julie walked into the kitchen, carrying several sheets of paper. "Save some for me," she cried, pointing to the cookie jar.

"Beat it!" Monica ordered.

"No way!" Julie stated. "We made a deal. I would look over your program for mistakes, and you would give me as many cookies as I wanted."

"Find any mistakes?" Monica asked.

"One. 'Hey, Jude' wasn't number one in nineteen sixty-six."

"She's right," Peter told her.

"When was it?" Monica asked.

Julie shook her head. "Where's my cookies?"

Monica dug out a handful of cookies and offered them to Julie, being careful to hand one to Peter first. "When was it number one?"

"It wasn't sixty-six." With that, Julie spun and left the kitchen while Peter laughed.

"I think I'm going to kill her!" Monica shouted.

Seeing the angry look on Monica's face was enough to make Peter stop laughing. "What difference does it make?"

"A lot. One of my listeners sent in a letter asking what year 'Hey, Jude' was number one. I was going to answer it on Sunday's show, after my interview with Brenda. What do you think?" Monica asked, and then quickly added, "I figured this way I can get a lot of the kids who listen to the show to write in. Then I'll get an idea of how I'm doing."

Peter looked at the cookie in his hand. His hunger disappeared. "Don't you think this whole thing is getting out of hand?" he asked, meeting her eyes at last.

"Wanting to find out the date of a song?" Monica replied, puzzled.

Remembering his talk with Brenda at Wolf-trap, Peter decided that it was time to bring up what was bothering him.

"No, not the song. You. Your show. That's all we talk about anymore. Every time I see you, every time we're together, we talk about your show."

Monica looked shocked. Shaking her head in denial, she blurted out, "We talk about the show because it's so important to us."

"Important to you, you mean," Peter corrected her.

Monica's jaw dropped. She stared silently at him for several seconds. "Peter," she whispered, her eyes filling with tears, "I'm sorry. I didn't realize it bothered you so much."

Peter looked at her, feeling a catch in his throat. When he spoke, his voice quivered. "It wouldn't bother me if you'd talk about something else once in a while!"

"I'm sorry," Monica repeated, shrugging her shoulders helplessly.

Peter swallowed hard. "Yeah, so am I. Look," he added trying to make his voice less harsh, "I'm in a rotten mood. I think I'd better just go home. Okay?"

A tear spilled from the corner of her left eye. "What time will you pick me up tonight?"

Peter watched the tear trace a slow path down Monica's cheek. His heart grew heavy. Reaching over to her, he wiped away the tear and forced his mouth into a large smile. "Eight?"

"I'll be ready," Monica promised.

Just try and forget about your show tonight, Peter asked her silently before turning and leaving the house.

"You have to make certain allowances for these things," Jonathan Austin said as he put down his coffee cup and gave Brenda a meaningful glance.

"How many times am I supposed to sit home because Brad has to work?" she challenged.

"He's a dedicated young man. There aren't too many boys like him anymore — you should appreciate that fact," Jonathan responded.

"Thank heaven," Brenda whispered louder than she'd intended.

"Brenda," her mother reprimanded.

"Sorry." But Brenda wasn't sorry, she was confused. And she couldn't talk to anyone about it. Her mother wouldn't understand what had happened between her and Jake in Rosemont Park; she wouldn't dare mention that to her stepfather. *And Chris?* Chris might try to understand, but Brenda knew that her stepsister was really too

150

straightlaced to be able to commiserate.

The only thing Brenda knew with any certainty was that she had to work out the situation by herself. "May I be excused?" she asked.

Her stepfather was about to say something, but her mother spoke first. "You can start on the dishes if you'd like."

Brenda stood, and Chris did, too. "I'll do them," Chris said with a wink.

"Thanks," Brenda said, relieved.

Chris mouthed: We'll talk later. Brenda nodded, left the dining room, and went straight through the kitchen and out the back door.

She walked across the neatly mowed lawn to the ancient wooden swing bench that her mother had brought with them when they'd moved into the Austin home. It had been the first of her mother's "things" that had been put up. Everyone enjoyed it now, but Brenda and Chris used it most often.

Sitting on the familiar yellow lacquered bench, Brenda dug her sneakers into the grass and pushed backward, and the old swing moved easily. She leaned back, trying to let the motion of the swing ease her stormy thoughts.

But a few moments later, she felt anything but calm. Jake's dark, hungry eyes haunted her, even though she had left him hours before. She remembered the softness of the grass beneath her back, and could almost feel his strong arms wrapped tightly around her. It had been as if she was the only thing in the world for Jake.

Jake needs me, damn it! she cried to herself.

He wasn't like Brad who obviously did not need her at all. In fact, Brenda realized sadly, Brad didn't seem to need anyone. Why couldn't you want me as much as I wanted you? she asked.

It wasn't until then that Brenda realized for the first time that she did, indeed, still want Brad. "I love Brad," she said out loud, almost as if she were trying to see how the words sounded. They didn't sound as empty as she'd thought they would.

Then how could I have let Jake kiss me and hold me? Brenda didn't have an answer to her question. She wondered if she ever would.

Suddenly, Jake's face rose up before her. His eyes smoldered, his face was stiff and angry, just as it had been when she had stopped him from kissing her any more. After telling him that she had to go home, Jake had gotten angry. He had wanted her to stay with him.

"I can't," she'd told him. "Not now."

"Because of your boyfriend?" he had asked angrily.

"No, because of me. Jake, I'm supposed to be helping you. I'm your counselor. I-I-It's not right for me to get involved with you emotionally," she had faltered.

Once again, the corner of his lip had quirked up. "Well, you're already involved with me emotionally."

"I can't think straight right now," she'd pleaded. "I have to go home."

"Sure, go run to your big house with all its fancy furniture. I'll go back to Garfield House and stare at the cracks on the ceiling."

Brenda felt stung by his sarcasm. "Jake, please, you're taking this the wrong way."

"Am I? You weren't kissing me like a counselor two minutes ago," he'd stated before turning and walking away.

I wasn't, was I? Brenda silently asked herself in an effort to stop the way she was torturing herself with what had happened in Rosemont Park. I really messed that up.

"Can I sit down with you?"

Brenda gasped when she looked up and saw Brad. Why had he come? Had he missed his seminar to be with her? She looked up at him with a question in her eyes.

Brad sat down next to her on the bench and put his arm around her shoulders. "Doctor Gordon was called into emergency surgery. His lecture was canceled."

Brenda felt a little spurt of anger, and wished he had lied to her just this once. "Oh," she whispered, trying her best to hide her disappointment.

"I'm so glad it was postponed. I needed to see you tonight, badly."

Gazing at his handsome face, Brenda knew that Brad was telling the truth. She also sensed that something was bothering him.

"I'm glad you came, too," she told him truthfully.

"Bren, something horrible happened today at the hospital," Brad began. Brenda nearly shut out his words when he said hospital, but the look of pain that darkened his eyes compelled her to listen.

"This afternoon I saw a seventeen-year-old boy die," Brad said in a choked voice.

Seeing the tired way his shoulders slumped, and the sad, faraway look in his eyes, Brenda's throat constricted. "How awful," she whispered.

Brad swallowed and nodded. "It was terrible. The doctor tried to save him, and worked fifteen minutes to get his heart started again, but it didn't do any good — the boy died just the same."

"What happened to him?" Brenda asked, impulsively taking Brad's hand and holding it tightly.

"He drove his motorcycle head first into a car. The policeman claimed that he was just driving wild and lost control of his bike. It happened in Cartwell. I. . . ."

"You what?" Brenda gently prompted.

Brad glanced away for a moment before gazing deeply into her eyes. For the first time, Brenda saw the dark circles of exhaustion under his eyes. "When I heard he was from Cartwell, I'd thought he might have been your friend Jake. But he wasn't.

"I — " Brad began but stopped to take a deep, shaky breath. "It scared me Brenda. He was only seventeen. He was our age! I kept looking at his face and thinking that it could have been me, or . . . or even you lying there. Oh, Brenda, I couldn't stand losing you."

Brenda's cheeks flamed scarlet with the sudden force of guilt that Brad's words produced. Releasing his hand, she looked away, ashamed that she had spent her afternoon kissing Jake in

Rosemont Park while Brad had been thinking of her.

"Bren," Brad called, reaching out to turn her face to him. "I also want you to know that I had an argument with my supervisor about the seminar. I tried to get out of it because I wanted to be with you."

Brenda felt overwhelmed by Brad's admission and more confused than ever. If he really did care about her, then was she wrong to feel this resentment? Was she demanding too much, expecting the impossible? Part of her still cared, though; maybe it wasn't too late.

Her fingers slid through Brad's neat brown hair, feeling the difference from when her fingers had glided through Jake's long, unruly hair. Pushing thoughts of Jake from her mind she kissed Brad, holding him close for several minutes. But she felt distanced from herself.

"I wish this were a deserted island — with just the two of us on it," she said wistfully.

Brad laughed. "You'd be bored to death."

"Maybe not," Brenda argued, lifting her head to gaze into his eyes. "At least I'd get to see you."

"You're seeing me now," Brad reminded her.

"I know."

"And don't forget Saturday night. I decided not to eat all day so I'd be ready for you," he proclaimed.

"I'll kill you if you pass out before you get here!" Brenda warned him sternly.

"Don't worry," Brad said with a smile, "I'll be here."

But for how long? Brenda wondered. If you leave me again, I can't predict what will happen. But her last thought before burying herself in his arms was of someone else.

Where are you now, Jake? Brenda wondered fearfully.

Chapter
16

"Not so hard, sweetheart," Brenda's mother suggested when she looked over her daughter's shoulder and saw the way Brenda was pounding the chicken breast.

"She's just pretending it's Brad's head, in case he has to work tonight," Chris teased.

"He won't be working tonight. It's Saturday night, and he promised," Brenda stated confidently. She looked at the meat hammer in her hand, before turning to her stepsister. "Or else," she added with a grin.

"Don't forget to add the quarter cup of white wine to the rice," Catherine Austin reminded Brenda as she snapped her purse shut.

"I won't, Mom, enjoy lunch at the club," Brenda said.

"And don't you forget to make sure that Ted is ready at six forty-five," she told Chris. "You know how annoyed your father gets if anyone is late."

"Ted will be ready, Catherine, I promise," Chris promised her stepmother. When Catherine Austin left the kitchen, Chris turned back to Brenda. "Need any help?"

Brenda shook her head. "I think I've got everything under control. What time are you picking Ted up?"

Chris glance at the wall clock. "I have to leave in a couple of minutes. Gee, I wish Ted and I were eating here tonight."

"I'll tell you all about it," Brenda promised.

"You'd better. I still can't believe you're doing all of this yourself."

Brenda looked at the now very thin chicken breasts. "Neither can I. Boy, am I becoming domestic."

"Not in that outfit," Chris said with a laugh.

Stepping away from the counter, Brenda looked down at herself. "What's wrong with it?" she asked.

Chris couldn't stop another low laugh from escaping. "I just don't think that pink leotards and an electric blue football jersey go with a yellow and orange flowered apron."

"Really?" Brenda asked innocently. "I never noticed."

"I'm sure it'll knock his socks off. But frankly, I don't think you need to work that hard to get Brad's attention. Well," Chris chuckled. "I've got to run. See you later."

"Wish Ted luck for me," Brenda called.

When the door closed, Brenda turned back to

the counter. She stared at the chicken, but didn't see it. Instead, she saw Jake's face floating in the air before her. A little while ago, she'd talked to Tony at Garfield House and he'd told her that Jake had moved out of the house Wednesday night — the very same day that she and Jake had spent the afternoon at Rosemont Park.

A foggy darkness had settled in her mind at the news that Jake had left Garfield House, but she had not let on to Tony how badly she was hurt. When she'd asked him where Jake had gone, Tony had said he'd moved in with a friend in Cartwell. It's all for the best, Tony had concluded. "Jake doesn't want our help. He was using us, Garfield House, as a crash pad."

Brenda hadn't argued with Tony, but she'd felt sick at heart because she knew *she* was responsible for Jake giving up on Garfield House.

"I was so stupid," she whispered, shaking her head in an effort to push away the shame of having to let her emotions for Jake take control of her. She was supposed to be his counselor, not his girl friend. But she hadn't acted like his counselor when they'd been at Rosemont Park.

If anything happened to Jake because of what she'd done, she would never forgive herself. "Never!" she stated.

Knowing that there was nothing she could do about Jake now, Brenda went back to work on the chicken breasts. When the two breasts were as flat and as wide as possible, she added the quarter cup of white wine to the simmering mixture of wild and long grain rice. After stirring it for two full minutes, she shut off the flame and set the pot aside. While the rice cooled, she unraveled a spool of cooking string, and cut two long pieces.

When the rice was cool enough to handle, she scooped several spoonfuls into the center of one breast and molded it with her fingers.

As she worked, she thought about the rest of the gourmet meal she had planned. The first course would be the French onion soup that was simmering on the back burner of the stove. After the soup, she would serve the chicken with the bright green string beans she had bought yesterday at the supermarket. She'd spent ten minutes picking through the crate, choosing only the most perfect ones. With the main course, she would also serve hot French bread and a salad. Later that afternoon she'd make a chocolate layer cake for dessert.

Smiling contentedly, she started to roll the chicken around the rice when the back doorbell rang. "It's open," she called and turned just as Kim Barrie stepped inside.

Coming close, Kim stared at the brownish mixture and then at Brenda. "Oh! Wow! Brenda, I think I'm gonna be sick!"

Brenda stepped quickly away. "It's just rice stuffing."

"Is that what you call it?" Kim asked, pointing to Brenda's colorful outfit, and not the rice.

Brenda couldn't stop a short laugh from escaping. "Very funny, but I've already heard about it from Chris." Then she noticed the white box in Kim's hand. "On a delivery?"

"Kind of. It's for you."

"Me?" Brenda asked in surprise.

Kim nodded happily. "I bumped into Brad yesterday morning when he was going in to work. He told me you were making a special dinner for just the two of you. Mom and I have a big job tonight, so I swiped a couple of strawberry tarts. I thought you might like them."

A rush of warmth flowed through Brenda. How thoughtful Kim was! "I'd love them. That's really great of you, Kim. Now I won't have to make dessert, and Brad loves your tarts. He had three of them at Monica's party."

"I'm glad. And Brenda. . . ."

"Yeah?"

"Can I give you some advice?" Kim asked.

Brenda did not miss the twinkle in Kim's eyes. "Such as?" she growled with mock sternness.

"Tonight. . . . Do you think that maybe you should ah . . . wear something a little quieter?" Kim asked with another broad smile.

Brenda raised her eyebrows before thoughtfully nodding her head. "You're probably right. Maybe Woody will loan me those new yellow suspenders you got him. They'll go good with iridescent green. Don't you think?"

Kim's eyes widened. "Right, great — have fun!" she added with another smile as she waved good-bye and started toward the door.

"Thanks again, Kim," Brenda said, her joking tone gone.

"Anytime," Kim replied warmly.

"Back to work," Brenda murmured after Kim was gone. When she had the two chicken breasts stuffed, rolled, and properly tied, she put them into the refrigerator, and retrieved the bag of string beans. In a low voice, she began to hum happily.

"Here's what I have in mind," Monica began. It was two-thirty P.M. and she and Brenda were discussing tomorrow's radio show. They talked for twenty minutes, Monica reading Brenda the different questions she had worked up for the show, and jotting down the answers Brenda gave her.

"That's about it," Monica said when she'd asked her last question. "We'll do fifteen minutes. When it's over, you can give out the phone number, address, and any other information you want."

"It sounds easy enough."

"It is, trust me," Monica said. "Is Chris around?" she asked suddenly.

"No. Ted has a game, and she's his cheering squad."

"Oh."

The tone of Monica's voice told Brenda that something was troubling her. "Is it important?"

Monica shrugged, but said, "Yes. I wanted to talk to her about Peter. He's acting really weird lately."

Brenda gazed intently at Monica. "I didn't think you noticed."

"How could I not notice? He's suddenly become so moody. It's like he's completely changed since the summer vacation started."

Brenda thought about herself and Brad, and

of all the plans that they had made and not kept. "Peter hasn't changed. You have."

"Me?" Monica echoed, her jaw dropping at Brenda's words. "How can you say that?"

"Listen to yourself sometime. Monica, since you became the Teen Beat disc jockey, you eat and sleep K-100. That's all you ever talk about. How many dates have you broken with Peter because of the show? And when you do go out, do you talk about what he did that day, or about what you're planning to do on your next show?"

"Well — " Monica began.

Brenda sighed. "Remember our double date together at Wolftrap?"

Monica's pale eyebrows knitted together. "Yes."

"Do you realize that while Brad was sleeping on my lap, you were writing down notes for your next show? You didn't even hear Peter when he complained to me about you."

"He complained to you?" Monica whispered, her cheeks turning scarlet.

"You were sitting right next to him. He wasn't whispering, either."

"I — "

"Monica, do you know how hard it must be for Peter to listen to you on the radio after spending two years trying to get that very job? I think he's shown a lot of self-control by not saying anything to you either. But you never give him a break. All you do is talk about *your* show."

Monica's eyes filled with moisture. She shook her head slowly. "It's not like that," she whispered. "I . . . I never thought about it that way."

"Does it make sense, though?" Brenda asked in desperation, trying to make her friend see the danger she and Peter were facing.

Monica nodded slowly. "I've felt like Peter's been growing distant. He not as . . . as loving anymore." Monica shrugged. "I just figured he had a lot on his mind."

"Stop making excuses. You sound like Brad. In fact, you've been acting like Brad for the last two weeks. Monica," Brenda said, her voice softening, "I'm not trying to get on your case, I just want you to see what's happening to you and Peter. And I'm taking Peter's side because I'm in the same position he's in."

"Because of Brad's job?" Monica asked.

"Yes," Brenda replied truthfully. "He's so wrapped up in it, I hardly see him anymore. But we're not talking about me, we're talking about you. And Monica, I'm sorry if you think I'm butting in, but I just had to say something. And I'm finished now, so I'll get my nose out of your business. What time are you picking me up tomorrow?" She asked with a smile, neatly changing the subject.

"Eight."

"A.M.?" Brenda squawked.

"The show's at ten. I have to be there by nine."

"I'll stay in my pajamas," Brenda warned.

"It's radio, not television. Dress any way you want," Monica said, her voice listless.

"Good," Brenda said. "And Monica, don't worry about what I said, do something instead. Make an effort tonight when you see Peter."

"I'm not seeing him tonight. He called this

morning, he's got a cold," Monica told Brenda as she closed her note pad and stood. "I'll see you in the morning. And Brenda, thanks for the talk. I . . . I really appreciate it. I'm going to do something about it, I promise."

"Good," Brenda said. As she stood up, she reached over to Monica, and hugged her friend tightly before saying good-bye.

Once Monica was gone, Brenda sat down at the table again. She was glad she'd had the nerve to speak her mind. At least one relationship might be salvaged now.

"The salad!" she cried, remembering that she'd gotten everything prepared except for the tomato and mozzarella salad. Standing, she started toward the refrigerator when there was a knock on the door.

"Now what?" she grumbled. "It's open?"

The door opened and Sasha Jenkins walked in. Sasha's long dark hair hung down to her waist, making her iridescent pink tank top glow. White shorts and hot pink sneakers completed the outfit.

"Hi, Sash, love your top."

"Hi, Brenda, thanks."

"Chris isn't here right now."

"I came by to see you," Sasha told her. "I brought you a book of poems I thought you might like to have for tonight."

"Poems?" Brenda asked.

"It's an anthology. Very romantic. For your dinner with Brad," Sasha added again.

Brenda smiled. "Chris told you about it, right?"

Sasha shook her head. "Brad told me when he

stopped by the bookstore yesterday. He's really looking forward to tonight."

"Thanks, Sasha, but does poetry go with stuffed chicken breast?"

"Romantic poetry goes with anything," Sasha assured her. "I'll just leave it here for you, in case."

"Okay, Sash, thanks again."

"Don't mention it. Say, I really love that top, can I borrow it sometime?"

"Anytime!" Brenda declared with a smile. "Anytime at all, and the leotards, too!"

After Sasha left, Brenda stared at the door for a long time, thinking how nice it was that Kim and Sasha had come over. She was touched by the gifts they had brought, and felt a special warmth for the girls she had once tried to ignore, but who had refused to let her ignore them.

Looking at the clock, Brenda saw she still had a couple of hours before Brad's arrival. She closed her eyes and thought about what she would do with her time. "A long, hot bubble bath first!" she declared, turning to leave the kitchen.

A hundred thoughts ran through her mind in a pleasant stream of anticipation. What she would wear tonight, and how she would do her hair were almost as important as deciding whether she would wear the new perfume she'd picked out yesterday, or the one Brad had given her for her birthday.

Filled with anticipation, Brenda raced upstairs.

Monica put down her pen and looked at the clock. It was exactly seven. She had finished the final draft of tomorrow's radio script, and had nothing to do for the rest of the night.

Sighing, she reflected on what Brenda had said earlier. She knew Brenda had been right, but it had taken her friend's forthright words to make her see that.

Monica closed her eyes, remembering the way Peter had acted the other day. He'd told her that all she did was talk about her show, only she hadn't been able to accept his words. She tried to think back to the other times she and Peter had been together during the last few weeks. Each time she remembered a date, she recalled that she had spent most of the time talking about Teen Beat.

"I never realized," she whispered, shocked that she had been so unfeeling toward Peter. No wonder he's been so cold to me.

Suddenly, she needed to see Peter. Going to the phone, Monica dialed his number. When she heard his voice, her heart skipped a beat. "Hi, it's me," she whispered.

Peter coughed loudly, and when he spoke his voice was raspy. "Is something wrong?" he asked.

His suspicious-sounding question puzzled her. It must be his cold. "No. I just wanted to speak to you. I miss you," she added quickly.

"I miss you, too," came the reply.

"Why don't I come over and take care of you?" Monica offered. "It'll be nice. I'll rent a movie and we can sit around and watch the tube."

"No," Peter said quickly. "You can't take a chance of catching whatever I have. *You* have a show to do."

"It's not that important," she told him.

Peter coughed loudly. "Yes it is," he said. "I'm sure this will be gone in a few days. I'll see you then."

"Peter," Monica called, her voice catching unevenly as she built up her courage to tell him she was sorry for what had been happening between them. But Peter didn't give her a chance.

"I've got to get back to bed, Monica. I'll listen to the show tomorrow. 'Night."

" 'Night," Monica whispered as she hung up the phone. Turning, she went back to the kitchen table and sat down. She stared at the script, but the words were too blurry to read. It took Monica several seconds to realize that her tears were making the ink run.

Peter hung up the phone, went back to the couch, and switched the channel to MTV. He leaned his head back, while he watched an old video of David Bowie and Mick Jagger's "Dancin' in the Streets."

But he wasn't paying attention to the television, because all he could think of was Monica and her job. He hadn't liked lying to Monica. Peter didn't like lying at all. But he knew that if he had gone out with her tonight, all Monica would have talked about would have been tomorrow's show. He couldn't face that, which was why he'd told her he was sick.

Once again, Peter wondered whether he should break up with Monica, or try one more time to get through to her. "I don't know if I can," he said to the empty room.

Chapter
17

The dining room looked perfect. The oak table, covered by a pale blue lace tablecloth, held two place settings of the Austin's best china. The ivory plates were banded with hand-painted roses that gleamed in the candlelight.

Pale blue linen napkins, secured in the center by silver napkin rings, lay across the plates. Her mother's Gorham silver resided proudly next to the china. A small crystal vase, containing three white carnations, added the finishing touch to the table.

Smiling, Brenda started back to the kitchen to check on the chicken. As she passed the large wall mirror, she paused to look at herself.

Her pleated black high-waist pants were topped by an antique-ivory satin blouse. Her thick brown hair fell in glossy waves down to her shoulders. And she had put on dark blue eye shadow, which deepened her eyes. "I look nice," she told her image as she retucked her blouse, before heading into the kitchen.

Brenda glanced at the clock to see how much time was left before shutting the oven off. It was exactly seven forty-five. Praying that she had done everything correctly, Brenda went to check the chicken and opened the oven door.

The chicken was brown and crisp and smelled delicious. She shut the oven off and smiled to herself. But the smile turned to a frown when she looked back at the clock. Brad was supposed to have been there by seven-thirty — fifteen minutes ago, she realized.

"Come on Brad, don't be too late tonight," she pleaded.

As if on cue, the phone rang. Brenda stared at it, a premonition chilling her. She walked slowly over to the phone and, on the fourth ring, picked it up. "Hello?"

"Bren?" Brad asked.

Brenda closed her eyes tightly. "Where are you? You were supposed to be here fifteen minutes ago. Dinner is ready," she told him.

"Brenda, I've been trying to call you," he said.

"The phone hasn't rung in over an hour. Not since everyone left. Where are you?"

"I meant I haven't gotten a chance to call until now. I've been running around like crazy. Brenda, I . . . I don't know how to say this."

Brenda swallowed hard and turned to look at the oven and at the chicken inside it. "Say what, Brad?" she asked tersely, already certain of what he would say.

"I haven't been able to leave the hospital yet,"

he admitted. "When my shift ended, I was told I had to work the second shift because some of the guys called in sick."

Brenda sighed loudly, relieved that he was just going to be late. "What time are you coming over?" she asked, her voice a little brighter.

"Bren, I'm sorry," he said, his voice filled with apology. "I can't come over. I have to work until eleven tonight."

"You promised!" Brenda cried, unable to hold back the tears of frustration and disappointment that poured from her eyes. "You promised me, Brad. Why can't you get out of work tonight?"

"Because I can't. Brenda, I made a commitment when I took this job. I don't break my commitments. You should know that better than anyone," he told her in a defensive yet pleading voice.

"Should I?" Brenda asked with a sob she couldn't control. "What about the commitment you made to me? Or don't I count in your life anymore?"

"Brenda, I said I'm sorry. You know I wanted to be with you more than anything else, but — "

"Then you should be," she challenged, unwilling to listen to any more of Brad's apologies or excuses. "But it's too late now — we're finished!" she stated angrily and slammed the phone down. Slowly, with her hands covering her face, she sank to the floor and released all the tears and sadness within her.

A long time later, when Brenda finally had herself under control, she stood, wiped her tears on her satin sleeve, and looked at the oven.

"I'll show you, Brad Davidson!" she declared.

Moving with firm determination, she took the pan of chicken out of the oven and dumped it into the garbage. She did the same thing with the string beans. The tomato and mozzarella salad followed quickly.

She opened the refrigerator and took out the two strawberry tarts. She stared at them for several minutes and, with an angry smile on her face, lifted one and began to eat it. When she finished the first tart, she did the same thing with the second. "You deserve that!" she told her absent boyfriend.

But eating both of the pastries did not help ease her sorrow. Tonight was the last straw. Now Brenda knew for sure that Brad cared more about his job than he did about her. He was aware of how much work had gone into tonight's dinner. He also knew how much she had been looking forward to this special evening.

"Why couldn't you have loved me?" she whispered.

A few minutes later, the doorbell unexpectedly rang. At first Brenda wondered if it was the doorbell, or if there was some strange ringing in her ears. But when the bell rang for the second time, her heart speeded up and she quickly wiped her eyes.

"Brad," she half cried, hoping against hope that he had somehow gotten away from the hospital. A smile grew on her lips. She raced to the front door.

Opening it, her smile froze and her eyes widened. It wasn't Brad at all. It was Jake Hoover, wearing black jeans and his usual black T-shirt. He looked dark and mysterious, handsome and brooding as always. And, Brenda thought suddenly, sexy and dangerous and *perfect*!

"Hi," Jake said, a half smile on his lips. "Want to go for a ride?" He held up his left hand, from which two black helmets dangled by their straps.

"You always know when to show up, don't you?" Brenda asked.

Jake smiled as if he had always known she would come with him. His chiseled features looked strong and powerful in the hallway light. "I hope I do."

"Where have you been?" Brenda asked.

Jake shrugged. "At a friend's."

"Why did you leave Garfield House?"

Jake's dark eyes locked on Brenda's. His smile disappeared. "Because of you."

Brenda closed her eyes. "I'm sorry, Jake," she whispered.

Jake's hand reached out to cup Brenda's chin. "Don't be sorry, I'm back, aren't I?"

Jake's fingers were warm on her chin. Brenda didn't move from his touch. "At Garfield House?" she asked in surprise.

Jake shook his head. "Here. How about that ride?"

Brenda looked over Jake's shoulder. His bike was leaning on its kickstand in the driveway. The outside houselights glinted off the motorcycle, making it look dark and savage. A ride on that bike would be just right for the mood she was in. Brenda remembered Brad asking her never to ride on a motorcycle. He can't tell me

173

what to do! she thought angrily. "Yes, how about that ride?"

"All right!" Jake said. "Let's go."

After locking the front door, Brenda followed Jake to the bike. Her stomach fluttered nervously, but she pushed that feeling away. When Jake started the bike, the sound of its engine cut through the night. A chill of excitement raced along Brenda's spine as she climbed on the bike behind him.

Jake gunned the engine and her arms went around his chest. Leaning against his back, Brenda closed her eyes as they pulled away from the curb.

Minutes later Brenda opened her eyes. The warm summer air was cool on her face. The houses seemed to pass by like a picket fence. There was a feeling of freedom and speed, and Brenda laughed out loud delightedly.

Before she realized it, they were at Rosemont Park, where Jake pulled the bike to a stop near a thicket of trees. After helping her down from the bike, he led her over to one of the trees. Looking expectantly into her eyes, Jake put his arms around Brenda and drew her to him.

But Brenda tensed. She remembered the last time she and Jake had been to the park and how guilty she had been afterward. Then she thought of Brad's broken promise. Why shouldn't she enjoy herself with Jake? Tonight had made it all too obvious that Brad didn't care about her, and Jake did. Now when Jake kissed her, Brenda kissed him back. The never-forgotten thrill of

Jake's demanding kisses came back again. Her head spun dizzily; her heart pounded with excitement. Her breathing turned deeper and she had to force her mouth from Jake's.

Burying her face upon his shoulder, Brenda held Jake tight. "Why did you leave without telling me?"

"What was there to say?" Jake asked in a level voice.

Brenda looked up at him, but the dark night hid his features. "A lot," she whispered.

"This is how I speak," Jake told her, lowering his mouth to hers again.

The kiss lasted a long time. Then as Jake forced her down to the ground beside him, something snapped inside Brenda. She realized things were getting out of control. Be careful, one small but still sane part of her mind warned her. He's dangerous — too dangerous.

Brenda pulled away again, trying to control her racing heart. Pulling away from him, she quickly stood up. "Take me for another ride. Show me what it's really like to ride a bike!" she challenged him breathlessly.

The clouds that had been covering the moon parted. Silver moonlight washed over them. Jake looked wildly excited as he sprung to his feet. "You got it," he laughed, grabbing her hand and pulling her back to the bike.

After they had their helmets on, and Jake started the bike, he said, "Hold on."

Brenda secured her arms around Jake's chest. She locked her hands together just as he gunned the bike and released the clutch. The motorcycle spurted forward. The sound of the exhaust filled Brenda's ears.

He took the first turn hard and fast. Brenda almost screamed, but when the bike was moving in a straight line again, she breathed a sigh of relief.

"How's that?" Jake shouted back to her. For the first time, Brenda realized just how charged up he was. When he made the next turn even faster than the last, Brenda cried out.

"Easy," she pleaded.

"That *was* easy. You haven't seen anything yet," Jake told her as he shifted and accelerated. They were on the narrow, curving road that circled Rosemont Park. Brenda had been on the very same road a hundred times, but never at this speed. There were no street lights, and the darkness of the road, lit only by the motorcycle's single headlight, began to terrify her.

Ahead of them was a warning sign for another curve. Next to the sign, the speed limit was posted. Fifteen MPH, it read. "Slow down Jake," Brenda yelled into the wind.

Either Jake didn't hear her, or he ignored her, because instead of slowing down, he took the turn faster than ever. As they rounded the curve, Brenda saw a car's taillights ahead. Noticing that the car had its turn signal on and would therefore be turning into their lane, she relaxed, knowing that Jake would have to slow down.

But Jake didn't slow down. Instead, he accelerated. "Jake!" Brenda screamed just as Jake swerved past the car, narrowly missing it. From behind her came the angry blare of the car's horn.

"Slow down," she shouted, close to tears.

"Relax," he shouted back. "Enjoy the ride."

But Brenda couldn't enjoy the ride, she was too scared. And, she was becoming more frightened with every second.

In one crystal clear moment, Brenda understood what Tony had been trying to tell her. Jake was an outlaw, not because of what had happened to him at home, but because of what happened inside Jake's own head. Brenda suddenly remembered that Brad had watched a biker die. Brad had been worried for her.

"Slow down!" Brenda cried, feeling desperate. "Or let me off!"

"Relax," Jake repeated, "I know what I'm doing." Once again, he sped through a turn.

Halfway through the turn, a set of headlights appeared as a car drove, head first, out of a driveway. "Jake!" Brenda tried to scream, but no sound came out of her mouth.

To her horror, he again accelerated. Just when it looked as if they would hit the car, Jake swerved the black motorcycle sharply. Brenda thought she heard Jake laughing, but she wasn't sure, because suddenly everything in her world was moving in slow motion.

She caught a glimpse of the driver in the car, his eyes wide with surprise. She felt the bike skid and then wobble just as the car ran off the road and crashed into a telephone pole.

Jake's muscles tensed as he fought to control

the swerving bike. But an instant later, the bike was spinning sideways, the force of which threatened to tear Brenda's hands lose from Jake's waist.

Brenda felt a sickening jolt as the back wheel hit a pothole and then her grip was broken. She felt herself propelled into the air and reached out frantically for something to hold on to. There was nothing, though, only a roaring in her ears and a split second of terror before something hard struck her in the head.

Her breath was knocked from her chest before she could cry out. Darkness threatened to take her thoughts away. Brenda fought the darkness. She tried to move, but could not. She tried to open her eyes, but they would not obey her command.

Biting her lip hard, Brenda managed to open her eyes. The world swam in dark sickening circles. The strawberry tarts in her stomach turned sour. And then she saw Jake looking down at her.

"Are you all right?" she heard him ask.

Brenda tried to shake her head, but the effort made her dizzy. She tried to speak, to tell him that she hurt, but no words came out. And while she stared up at Jake, darkness covered her eyes and took him away.

Brad hung up the phone and retrieved his quarter. He had been calling Brenda every fifteen minutes for the past hour and a half. But she had not answered the phone once.

Brad stared at the clock. Its hands read nine-fifteen. Ever since Brenda had hung up on him, he'd been miserable. He'd asked himself a hundred times why he hadn't said no to Mr. Greer, when his supervisor had asked him to work the second shift. "Because I'm stupid," he told himself, hoping that tonight had not completely destroyed their relationship.

Brad could have said no. He had already worked two double shifts in the past two days. But he had told himself that he was needed at the hospital, and that was more important.

"Important for my big head," he said as Brenda's angry parting words filled his head again. "We're through!" she had said.

Suddenly, Brad knew he had to go to Brenda and apologize, if it wasn't already too late. Turning, he went to look for his supervisor, and found Mr. Greer in the emergency room.

"Mr. Greer," he called, steeling himself for their confrontation. This time, however, he would not take no for an answer.

"Yes, Davidson?"

Before Brad could speak, the ambulance entry doors burst open and two paramedics rushed a new patient inside. "Just a minute," Supervisor Greer said to Brad as he went over to them. "What happened?" he asked.

"Motorcycle accident. The driver of the bike left the scene and his passenger. There was another car involved. The driver of the car called us. There was no identification on the girl," the paramedic reported.

"Put her over there," the nurse instructed the paramedic, pointing to the examining table in the cubicle near Brad. As the paramedics moved the gurney, the nurse picked up the phone and paged the emergency room doctor.

When the gurney came toward him, Brad looked down at the girl. His heart froze. The blood drained from his face. "No!" he cried, his voice filled with anguish.

"What's wrong, Davidson?" Supervisor Greer asked, turning quickly to look at Brad. "Do you know her?"

Brad held on to the side of the gurney. He stared down into Brenda's closed eyes. "She's — Brenda Austin. She's — she's my girlfriend."

Slowly, Brad bent. Tears filled his eyes as he brushed away a patch of dirt from Brenda's cheek. "What happened?" he asked her.

As he spoke, Brenda's eyes fluttered open. "Brenda?" Brad cried softly. But she didn't answer. It was then he realized her eyes were glazed — she wasn't seeing him at all.

"I . . . I'm so sorry," he whispered as he kissed her lips. "I love you, Brenda. Please," he prayed hoarsely, "please be okay."

Chapter
18

Monica arrived at K-100 at eight forty-five Sunday morning and went to the desk she had been given. There, she took out the program script she had spent all week working on, and rewrote it as best she could, before showing it to her supervising DJ for him to approve the changes.

But her mind was filled with so many different things, that she couldn't concentrate on what she was doing. She had learned about Brenda's accident late last night. She had also learned that Peter had not been sick.

Monica accepted the blame for Peter's lie. In fact, she had spent the entire night thinking about her behavior these past few weeks and had come to the conclusion that everything her friends had been trying to tell her was true.

She had been thoughtless and selfish, never once considering Peter's feelings, or the fact that he might have been jealous about her good luck. How could I? All I ever thought about was the next show.

And, poor Brenda. Instead of laughing and having fun on her show today, Brenda was in the hospital with a concussion and sprained ankle and wrist. When she'd spoken to Chris earlier, Chris had said that Brenda was lucky, she could easily have been killed.

When she'd asked why Brenda had been out with someone on a motorcycle when she was supposed to be having dinner with Brad, all Chris had said was that Brad had canceled their date.

"Brad was stupid," Monica whispered, "just like I've been with Peter."

Picking up the phone, Monica dialed Peter's number. She desperately needed to apologize — if it wasn't already too late. When Peter's mother answered the phone, Monica asked to speak to Peter. Mrs. Lacey left to get Peter, but when Monica heard the phone picked up again, it was Mrs. Lacey who spoke.

"I'm sorry, Monica, Peter said he doesn't feel well enough to talk right now."

"Does he know I called when he was out last night?" she asked.

"Yes, I told him when he came in."

"Thank you," Monica whispered before she hung up.

Closing her eyes, she willed herself not to cry. Taking a deep breath, she picked up the phone and called Kim. The second she heard Kim's voice, she explained what had happened. "Go over to Peter's, please," she begged Kim. "Make him listen to the show today. It's important, Kim. Very important."

When Kim promised to go over to Peter's, Monica hung up, picked up her pencil, and began to write like crazy.

Where am I?

Brenda had a terrible headache, and she was hearing voices. She remembered fleeting images: Jake, Brad, a lot of people in white clothing, and Brad again. She opened her eyes and found everything was blurry. She blinked several times until the white ceiling came into focus.

She turned her head just enough so that she could see her mother and stepfather standing near the window. They were talking in low voices. When she turned her head to the other side, she saw Chris sitting next to the bed, frowning and looking down at her lap.

Brenda moistened her dry lips with her tongue. "H-hi," she whispered.

Chris's head snapped up. She leaned forward, a hesitant smile replaced her frown. "Hi, yourself. Welcome back."

"What . . . what happened?" Brenda asked.

"Oh darling, don't you remember?" Brenda's mother asked, rushing over to the bed. She stroked Brenda's forehead, gently, tears in her eyes.

Brenda closed her eyes again. Suddenly, the night came back. She saw the car coming out of the driveway. She felt the bike sliding and spinning and remembered the horrible sensation of flying through the air. "I remember," she admitted in a hoarse whisper.

"We've been so worried about you," Jonathan Austin said.

"I . . . I feel so foolish," Brenda said as a wave of dizziness washed across her, forcing her to close her eyes for a moment.

"At least you're going to be okay," her stepfather added, leaning over to squeeze her hand. "And that's the important thing. We'll talk about what happened later, when you're up to it."

Brenda smiled her thanks to Jonathan, and squeezed his hand in return.

"Yes, that's a good idea," her mother told her as she bent and kissed Brenda on her cheek. "We'll be back later," she promised before turning to Chris. "Chris?"

Chris shook her head. "I'm going to stay for a while."

When Chris and Brenda were alone, Chris pulled her chair closer. "You had us all scared to death. You should have seen us at the Courtlands'. They had just served the main course when we got the call from the hospital. What happened?" she asked suddenly.

"Brad canceled. He had to work again," Brenda said.

Chris nodded. "I know Brad had to work, but how did you end up on a motorcycle? And who were you with? Jake Hoover?"

Brenda's eyes widened. "You don't know?"

Chris shook her head. "All we know is what Brad told us. He was here when they brought you in. That's why the hospital was able to reach us at the Courtlands'. He stayed with you all night."

A misty vision filled Brenda's eyes. It was the dream she'd had before opening her eyes and finding her parents in the room. It had been of Brad. He had been with her, holding her and talking gently to her. She had even felt his lips on hers. Had it been a dream? she wondered.

"Wh-what about Jake?" Brenda whispered.

Chris stared at a spot just over Brenda's head. When she spoke, her voice was sharp with anger. "The driver of the car told the police that the boy riding the motorcycle checked to make sure you weren't dead, and then asked him to call an ambulance. When the man went into his house, the biker — I guess it was Jake — picked up his bike and disappeared. He didn't even wait to find out how badly you were hurt."

Chris's words stunned Brenda. She couldn't believe Jake had abandoned her like that. Slowly, she tried to tell her stepsister what had happened, but the pounding in her head was too much. "My head hurts."

"It should. You have a concussion, and you sprained your left wrist and right ankle."

"Chris, I'm sorry."

"Oh, Brenda, we're — I'm just so glad you're okay," Chris whispered softly, her voice thick with emotion.

"I was mad at Brad for canceling our dinner date," Brenda said. "And so when Jake showed up and asked me if I wanted to go for a ride, I accepted." When she paused to look into Chris's eyes, she was surprised to see a look of empathy.

Chris wasn't critical as she'd expected — she understood!

Chris smiled. "I understand why you did that, Bren, I really do."

Tears filled Brenda's eyes. She reached out for Chris's hand and, when she touched it, she clasped it hard. "Thank you."

They gazed at each other for several moments before Chris broke the stare to look at her watch. "It's ten o'clock." Brenda looked confused.

"Sunday, ten o'clock," Chris repeated.

"Oh no," Brenda half cried. "Monica's radio show."

"Well, at least you still have your memory," Chris joked as she picked up the portable radio she'd brought to the hospital and placed it on the bed stand.

Just as she turned it on, the nurse came in. "Time for your medication," she told Brenda. After giving the pills to Brenda, she looked at Chris. "I think your sister needs some rest now. Why don't you come back later?"

Chris stood and kissed Brenda's cheek. "I'll be back," she promised. "Listen to Monica's show."

When she was alone again, Brenda listened to the opening of Teen Beat. After the first song was over, Monica came on the air.

For a moment, Brenda didn't realize what Monica was saying. Then as her friend's words soaked in, tears pooled in her eyes. Monica was telling the radio audience that the guest who had been scheduled to be on Teen Beat had been in a motorcycle accident, and was in the hospital.

"But," Monica announced, "I'm sure she'll be

on the show next week, so she can tell all of you about the great work that's being done at Garfield House. And now, because Brenda is such a special person, not just to me and to her friends and classmates at Kennedy High School, but to all the kids who look up to her and depend on her at Garfield House, I'd like to give Brenda my prayers, and offer Brenda, and her boyfriend, Brad, this Billy Joel song, 'Everyone Has a Dream.'

"And remember, all of you out there, dreams can come true, but you have to work to make them happen."

Brenda sobbed out loud when Monica stopped talking and Billy Joel's voice took over. But the medicine the nurse had given her had started to make her sleepy, and just before the song ended, Brenda fell into a deep, restful sleep.

"That was really nice," Peter said after noisily clearing his throat. "I only wish Monica could listen to her own advice."

"Have you given her a chance?" Kim asked as Billy Joel's voice filled the room. She was sitting next to Peter in the Lacey's family room. It had taken a lot of effort on her part to get Peter to listen to Monica's show; Kim only hoped it would all be worth it.

"How can I? She doesn't stop talking about her show long enough for me to say anything to her, unless it's about her show."

"Is that why you lied to her last night?"

Peter looked away from her. "No. Yes," he admitted. "I need to think."

"About what?" Kim asked.

187

"About whether to break up or not," he admitted.

Kim sighed. She had been afraid of that. "I thought you loved Monica."

"I do. I love the Monica who came to me looking for a job as my assistant. Not the hotshot she's become."

"You know, Peter, everyone changes," Kim argued. "They can't always stay the same."

Peter smiled at Kim. "No, they can't. But sometimes the change a person goes through isn't for the best." He paused to take a deep breath before continuing.

"And I have to admit that I was jealous. I would have been jealous of anyone who had gotten the job I wanted. But I'm not jealous anymore. I can live with the fact that I didn't get the job and Monica did. What I can't handle is her insensitivity. When we go out, I'm out with a radio show, not my girl friend. She never lets me forget how great she is, and how great her show is." When Kim didn't say anything, Peter continued, "How would you like it if Woody decided to become a caterer and — "

"Don't say any more," Kim pleaded, "I understand what you mean."

"Good. But I — "

"Wait!" Kim cried, pointing to the radio.

Peter sighed and shook his head as Monica's voice came through the speakers.

"I've received some great letters from you guys and girls out there telling me how much you've liked my first show. And I really appreciate it. But I think it's time you found out that it's not just the disc jockey who is responsible for making a radio show a success. A radio show is the work of a whole bunch of people from the program director, to the station manager, to the office staff, and especially to Howard Thompson, my engineer.

"For those of you who don't know what an engineer does, I'll make it simple. Without an engineer, there wouldn't be a show. It's the engineer who makes sure that everything is working right, and that what I say or play gets to you folks out there in radio land.

"So you see, I'm the last one who should get any credit," Monica stated. "Because without all these people helping me, I wouldn't be able to do my job. But, there's one more very important person I have to mention. It's this person who is more responsible than anyone else for making my show as good as it is. Without this person's help, I don't think any of you out there would be listening to me."

"Annie Ross," Peter said with a shake of his head. "She's the one responsible for her getting the job."

Kim grabbed his wrist tightly. "Please, Peter. Please listen." And, seeing the look on Kim's face, Peter listened.

"Without his guidance and wisdom and experience, I could never have pulled Teen Beat together. He taught me what it means to be more than just a voice coming out of a speaker. His name is Peter Lacey, and he's my boss at WKND radio at Kennedy High, and he is the best disc jockey in the world. I love you, Peter," she said just as she segued into the new Duran Duran single.

"Oh, wow," Peter whispered.

"Annie Ross?" Kim asked.

"Cool it, Barrie," he said gruffly, "I need to think." Turning away from Kim, Peter stared at the wall. He couldn't look at anyone right then. It wouldn't be right for Kim to see the tears in his eyes.

Chapter 19

The second time Brenda awakened, Monica's show had been over for quite a while. The first thing she realized was that she felt much better. Her head no longer hurt as badly as before.

Opening her eyes slowly, Brenda found everything in focus. She looked at the small clock her mother had left on the bed table, and saw it was almost two o'clock.

"Hi," came Brad's voice.

Turning, Brenda saw Brad standing near the foot of the bed. He had dark circles under his eyes, and although he was smiling at her, his mouth was drawn and tense.

"Hi," Brenda replied in a low voice.

"I brought this for you," Brad said. He came around to the side of the bed and handed her a single long-stemmed white rose nestled within emerald green ferns. When Brenda took the beautiful flower from him and sniffed its heady fragrance, Brad went on.

"Brenda, I'm really sorry about what happened last night. It was my fault, all of it. Can you ever forgive me for being such a fool?"

Brenda looked up at him. Her eyes misted, and Brad's features blurred. She tried to speak, but confusion blocked her voice. Shame for what she had done last night tempered her thoughts, but did not soften the knowledge that she was still terribly upset with Brad for having broken his promise.

"It wasn't your fault," she said unconvincingly.

"Yes it was!" Brad declared. Turning, he walked toward the door. His back was rigid and tense, and when he looked back toward her, she saw that his face was full of pain and self-reproach.

Before she could speak, Brad strode purposefully back to her bed, gripped the railing, and gazed down at Brenda. "If I had been as concerned about you as I was about my job, you wouldn't be here now. But I wasn't. So it was my fault, Brenda."

Brenda had never seen Brad like this before. His words were compelling. But after all the broken dates and promises, she was afraid to believe that he meant what he said.

"It will never happen again, I promise you that it won't," Brad said, pulling up a chair close to the bed. "I'd like to stay with you for a while, if I may."

"I'd like that, too," Brenda said, unsure about what she was really feeling for him.

"But you've got to rest, also. Just close your eyes and relax while I get a vase to put the rose in."

Brenda did as he asked, but after he left, a myriad of thoughts burst into her head. Pictures of Brad and Jake floated before her eyes. Why had Jake left her like that and where had he gone?

"Did you know you're the prettiest girl in Rose Hill?" Brad asked, jarring her thoughts.

Brenda opened her eyes to see Brad framed in the doorway, holding a hospital water pitcher in his left hand. The way the light from the window struck his face made Brenda remember just how handsome he was. "I don't think that's true. And . . . and especially in this yucky white hopsital gown," Brenda replied shyly.

"Trust me, it's true," he added as he came over to the bed, and took the rose from her hand and put it in the pitcher. "They don't have vases," he explained.

"It's beautiful anyway."

"Thank you."

Brenda gazed at Brad, and for the first time realized that he was wearing his orderly uniform. "Are you on a break?"

Brad shook his head. "I'm not working today. I — I spent the night here," he hesitantly admitted. "I haven't gone home yet, and I wore my uniform to work yesterday."

"Oh, Brad," Brenda whispered, remembering her dreams, and what Chris had told her earlier. Now she knew she hadn't been dreaming. It had been Brad who had kissed her and had been with

193

her during the night. "I'm so sorry," she said, holding back a sob.

"Don't be," Brad told her quickly. "I know this sounds crazy, but maybe what happened last night was for the best. Because. . . ."

Brad's voice caught roughly, and he looked away from Brenda for a moment. Brenda reached for his hand, and when her smaller fingers wrapped around his larger ones, she asked, "Because what?"

"Because," Brad said, swallowing, "it showed me how dumb I could be. I . . . I put this job ahead of us. I was afraid that if I didn't do well here, that somehow I would mess up things for the future. Did I do that?" he asked.

Brenda had to blink quickly to hold back her tears. "I . . . I don't know," she admitted.

"I hope not, Bren. I really do love you," he told her, standing closer to her.

Brenda looked up into Brad's warm eyes. "I love you, too, Brad," she whispered.

"Last night you said we were finished," Brad said.

"I said and did a lot of foolish things last night," Brenda admitted. "And I —" But Brad cut her next words off with a kiss.

When he straightened up he smiled at her. "You don't have to explain yourself to me. And, things are going to be better for the rest of the summer. I promise, Brenda. And this time I won't forget what's most important — you."

"Thank you," she whispered.

Brad smiled. "I'm going home to change. But I'll be back, for you, not for work," he said as he turned and went to the door. Pausing, he glanced back over his shoulder at her. "Should I send Chris up? She's still in the waiting room."

"Please," Brenda said as she waved good-bye again.

After he was gone, Brenda continued to think about what Brad had said. Strangely, Brad's words had somehow opened a door in her mind which she had been keeping shut.

She saw just how unfair she had been in her anger toward Brad. Maybe it was because she was used to his being strong, the one person who was always there for her when she needed him. She remembered one day during finals, when she'd been at her wit's end trying to get ready for a test, and Brad had come over to help her. She had called him her Rock of Gibraltar. But when he had started work at the hospital, and had kept breaking their plans and dates, she felt he'd deserted her. He was no longer there when she needed — and wanted him.

She thought about what Brad had told her a few minutes ago. He had said that he was afraid if he didn't do well at the hospital, that somehow he would mess up things for the future. Brenda had heard words like those more times than she wanted to remember. A lot of kids at Garfield House said similar things. It was insecurity that was behind their words.

In a moment of absolute clarity, Brenda saw Brad as he really was, not as she had tried to make herself believe he was. He was human and, like all the other kids, he had his insecurities, too. Only Brad had been able to hide them from her.

Everything was making better sense to Brenda: Brad had been the student council president; he had been the overachiever in everything. Brad was so insecure that he had to constantly prove that he was the best. He devoted all his energy to doing this so that no one would know he was afraid he might not measure up to other people's standards.

"You just have to measure up to your own standards, Brad," Brenda whispered. "Those are the important ones."

"This is really pretty," Chris said, going over to the rose. "Brad, huh?" she asked, sniffing delicately at the white petaled flower.

"Brad, huh," Brenda replied with a smile. "You knew he gave it to me, didn't you?"

Chris nodded. "He was really broken up about what happened."

"It wasn't his fault." This time Brenda believed her words.

"In a way it was. You were depending on him and he let you down."

"I was wrong, I shouldn't have depended so *much* on Brad. I should have depended on myself, too. And I should have been able to understand what Brad was going through." Brenda paused and then asked the question that had been edging its way into her mind. "Have they found Jake yet?"

Chris shook her head. "Not that I know. But they're still looking for him, and so the police may be by later. Don't try to protect him, okay?"

"I won't," Brenda promised. "Guess that means he hasn't come to the hospital."

196

"Are you kidding?" Chris asked, her face reflecting shock that Brenda would even think such a thing. "If he left you on the road, why would he show up here? Besides," she added, "I had the impression that you and Brad patched things up."

Brenda eyes lit up. "We did. And now that Brad and I *both* know he's not Superman, maybe we can really be happy."

"No more Jake?"

Brenda shook her head. "No," she whispered. "I . . . I just wanted to know if he was all right."

Chris shrugged. "No one ever knows if guys like Jake are ever all right. At least I don't."

An instant later, they heard loud voices. Chris jumped up, startled by the cry, while Brenda smiled at the five kids who were all trying to push through the doorway at the same time.

"Yo! Paging Mrs. Evel Knievel," Woody Webster repeated from the back of the pack.

Brenda watched her friends parade into the room, and was surprised to see Peter and Monica holding hands and smiling warmly at each other. They looked like they were in love again.

Ted walked over to Chris, kissed her cheek, and then took off his baseball cap and put it on Brenda's head. "You need something to cheer you up," he told her. "We made first place yesterday. And that," he added, pointing to the red billed hat Brenda wore, "was responsible for the winning run."

"I knew it wasn't you," Woody teased warmly, "but I never figured it was a hat that hit the ball."

"Watch it, Webster," Chris warned, punching Woody playfully on his shoulder.

"Sorry I missed your show," Brenda said to Monica.

"I figured you got stage fright and thought that flying off a motorcycle was better than having to talk on the radio. But," Monica added with a stern look, "you still have to do the interview!"

"I will," Brenda promised, "and thanks for what you said on your show."

"Did you hear what else she said?" Peter asked.

Brenda shook her head. "They gave me some medicine and I fell asleep right after Billy Joel."

"Wow!" Woody chimed in, looking around the hospital room. "Was he here, too?"

Everyone laughed.

"What else did you say about me?" Brenda asked Monica.

Monica turned red. She looked up at Peter. "It wasn't about you. It was about Peter. I . . . I guess I told him how much of a dummy I've been."

Brenda was pleased to hear Monica's words. "I'm glad."

"Me, too," Peter said.

"Excuse me," came the authoritative voice of a nurse. "There are only four visitors allowed in a patient's room at one time, not six."

"Booo!" Woody said before Kim put her hand over his mouth.

Chris smiled at Brenda. "Want me to stick around?"

Brenda shook her head. She needed to be alone for a little while. "I'm getting pretty tired," she told Chris and the others. "You guys go on and have some fun today."

"We'll be thinking of you," Kim said.

"Thanks," Brenda replied, meaning it.

Under the watchful eyes of the nurse, Brenda's stepsister and five friends filed out of the room. When they were gone, Brenda sank back into her pillows. She had never realized before how important her friends had become to her. It was a nice feeling, but it also scared her a little, too.

"Since when does my favorite girl wear a hat to bed?" Tony Martinez asked, entering the room. "Or is that what happens when you do a swan dive onto the blacktop?"

Brenda smiled with pleasure at seeing Tony. "Hi, boss."

"Everyone at the house wanted to come with me. But I convinced them that I would bring back a glowing report. Can I?" he asked, his warm eyes filled with concern.

"I'm fine," Brenda told him. "Just a couple of sprains and a concussion."

"It's not the sprains or the concussion I'm worried about, it's here, and here," he said, pointing first to his temple, and then to his heart. "Want to talk about it?"

"Have you heard from Jake?" she asked.

Tony exhaled sharply. "Not exactly. The police came by Garfield House looking for him. I sent them to the address Jake gave us. The officer came back later and told us Jake was gone. No one knows where."

"I see," Brenda whispered, looking away from Tony.

"You haven't answered me. Want to talk about it?"

Brenda sighed and stared at the foot of the bed.

"It's okay if you don't want to talk about it," Tony told her, his voice warm and reassuring. "I've been in your place myself. Anyone who tries to help other people gets caught up sometime. It's not hard to get emotionally involved when you're trying to be the first one to touch that place where no one else has ever been able to reach. Things happen then, that we don't expect."

Brenda nodded to Tony. "I'm okay, Tony. I . . . I've learned my lesson. No more outlaws."

Tony favored Brenda with a wide smile. "That's important," he said as he bent and kissed her brow. "Get better quick. We need you at Garfield House, and don't ever forget that."

"I won't," she promised.

When she was alone again, Brenda tried to tell herself that she really was okay, and what she had told Tony was the truth. She had learned her lesson, and she would be careful in the future. Right?

Now the comparisons she had been making before, between Jake and Brad, came back to her. This time she saw them in a different light.

Jake was the sort of guy who showed up only when he felt like it. He left the same way. Brad wanted responsibilities, Jake ran from them. Brad genuinely cared about people. Jake was an outlaw who cared only for himself.

"I'm better off without him," Brenda said aloud

as a picture of Brad, smiling and holding his arms out to her, filled her mind.

And she was certain now, too, that she and Brad would make things work out. Maybe, Brenda thought with a smile, her feelings for Brad ran even deeper than she'd realized. Sometimes something had to happen to a relationship before a couple realized just how good they had it.

Not even the haunting image of Jake Hoover's brooding face and eyes could dampen her soaring spirit. The memory of the times they had kissed so passionately rose up to challenge her newfound determination to make things work out with Brad.

"No," she told Jake's image. "Not this time." And with her denial of Jake, something inside her changed. She discovered a strength that she had not known she possessed. It came, she realized, from a feeling of maturity which allowed her to think of Jake, even though she loved Brad.

I do love Brad, she told herself truthfully. But I have my memories of Jake, too.

Smiling, Brenda closed her eyes, and as sleep crept slowly over her, she pictured herself walking hand in hand with Brad beneath the golden summer sun.

Coming Soon . . .
Couples No. 13
CHANGING PARTNERS

The front door to the Albatross was propped open to let in the warm, sweet summer breeze, so Sasha didn't hear the bell that usually alerted her to a customer's entrance. Instead she was aware she was no longer alone in the store when a movement a few aisles away caught her eye. She looked up.

It was a boy, or rather a young man. He definitely looked older than the Kennedy crowd. He was tall and tanned, and his sandy hair was a little bit long and curly around his neck. He was wearing cutoff jeans and a faded orange T-shirt. And though he was wearing glasses, they couldn't hide the brightness of his hazel eyes.

Sasha caught his eye and smiled inquiringly, but he just smiled back and started working his way around the stacks until he reached the history section. Sasha left him alone — browsers were always welcome at the Albatross. She looked back down at her book. She'd read just one more page . . . okay, she'd finish the chapter. Sasha jumped. The sandy-haired boy was standing in front of her, his bright hazel eyes smiling down at her.

"Do you need some help?" she asked.

He squatted beside her and smiled. "If you're supposed to be unpacking these cartons, it looks like you're the one who could use some help. Let me give you a hand."

Sasha had closed *The House of Mirth* and now he took the book gently from her hands. "Edith Wharton, hmm? She was really something else. It's a shame some writers can't be immortal."

It was always nice to talk to somebody who felt the same way she did about books. Her friends tended to roll their eyes when she got started on her favorite author. "Yeah, when I heard that she'd died, I thought about wearing a black armband!"

"I know what you mean," he said. "When E. B. White died, we flew the flag at half mast at my school."

She grinned. "You *did*? I grew up on *Charlotte's Web*. That sounds like a neat school."

"It is," he said pushing a thick lock of hair back from his eyes. "I'm lucky to go to a college that offers so much."

Sasha felt a tingle at the base of her spine. She'd guessed he was older, but somehow the word "college" made her look at him with new eyes. Still, he didn't make her feel at all shy; she leaned forward, her elbows on her knees, hoping he'd continue.

WINNERS

by Suzanne Rand

A great new mini-series from the publishers of *Sweet Dreams*.

Being seventeen can be great fun – as Stacy Harcourt, Gina Damone and Tess Belding discover as they enter their exciting senior year at Midvale High School. Apart from years of friendship, the popular trio share their main interests in common – an obsession with cheerleading in the elite school squad, and boys! For all three girls, the intricate gymnastic jumps and routines of their favourite hobby are the best things in their lives – but the gorgeous footballers they are supporting are definitely the icing on the cake! Picked to lead the cheering, the girls know they have one of the school's highest honours and a big responsibility to be the best that they can be in every way.

Each book highlights the story of one of the girls.

1. THE GIRL MOST LIKELY
2. ALL AMERICAN GIRL
3. THE GOOD-LUCK GIRL

WINNERS – available wherever Bantam paperbacks are sold!